"I don't think of you as my mistress."

Max's voice sounded dazed as he went on. "Why won't you marry me?" Sophie shook her head helplessly. "So you don't love me as I love you," he said flatly.

"Do you love me?" she whispered.

"Yes," he said roughly. "The rest of my life is hardly enough time to spend with you."

She couldn't believe it. He was offering her what she most wanted. But marriage with Max was not for her. She could love him, have an affair with him. But not marriage.

Maximilian von Hartog had a title and an inheritance to pass on. He could not marry a nameless girl born of unknown, unmarried parents.

"I can't give you what you want," she said slowly, "and you can't accept what I can give. Perhaps we're better apart...."

D0451272

SUSAN ALEXANDER was born and lived in Hanover, Germany, until her family settled in England when she was nine. They traveled widely, and after attending Oxford University, she gave in to her passionate desire to work in the world of feature films. Success in the movie community came at the cost of her marriage and family life, and she feels that writing has become the most engrossing part of her life outside her family—which includes a new husband. "I consider myself extraordinarily fortunate," she says. "I believe I have experienced everything any woman could possibly wish for herself."

Books by Susan Alexander

HARLEQUIN PRESENTS
499—WEDDING IN THE FAMILY
719—THE MARRIAGE CONTRACT
807—TEMPORARY HUSBAND

SUSAN ALEXANDER

winter sunlight

Harlequin Books

TORONTO • NEW YORK • LONDON
AMSTERDAM • PARIS • SYDNEY • HAMBURG
STOCKHOLM • ATHENS • TOKYO • MILAN

Harlequin Presents first edition December 1987
Second printing November 1987
ISBN 0-373-11031-6

Original hardcover edition published in 1987
by Mills & Boon Limited

CHAPTER ONE

'No,' Sophie Carter said adamantly.

'But, Sophie darling, it's tailor-made for you.'

The older woman leaned back in her leather chair and looked up at her. She had a long way to look, because Sophie was very tall indeed. Nor was she exactly thin as a reed. Her voluptuous figure was generously proportioned and topped by a vivid face. Below the thick, luxuriant black hair, that face was not beautiful. Large eyes of a nondescript hazel, a straight nose, a mouth too full for symmetry and a chin given to determined stances all added up to what Sophie herself derided as plain, ignoring the creamy skin and the light eyes that could flash with anger or mischief, revealing tiny flecks of tawny yellow. Her height gave her a commanding presence, and Sophie was used to getting her own way.

The silence lengthened as the two women looked into each other's eyes. It was Sophie who first dropped her gaze.

'There are times, Lottie Ritter, when I positively dislike you,' she announced, and sat down.

'I know dear, and I realise I'm being difficult, but it would be so . . .'

'No,' Sophie said for the second time.

The older woman reached for a cigarette from a silver box on the desk in front of her.

'Sometimes I wonder if I really understand you,' she said slowly.

'I thought you knew us all so well you could

practically hear us think,' retorted Sophie drily.

'And now I've made you angry,' said Lottie quietly, 'which is the last thing I wanted.'

Her voice was soft, the slight, guttural sound of her foreign origin only faintly discernible in her pronunciation. With her vivid red hair she successfully disguised how old she was. The pale, wrinkled face and slightly arthritic hands revealed her to be pushing seventy, but the sprightly energy and the lively curiosity in the small brown eyes more than made up for the bottle-coloured hair and heavy make-up.

As she watched her insert the cigarette into an ancient tortoiseshell holder, Sophie's face softened. She owed Lottie more than she could ever repay. Five years ago, she had first walked into the tiny cramped office with its huge antique desk, its ancient black typewriter and its mountains of files perching on tables and spilling to the floor in all corners of the room. Her Norland nanny diploma clutched in her hand, Sophie had been shy and awkward, desperately conscious of her height and what she considered her total lack of attraction.

Lottie had taken her on, and in the months that followed had coaxed and bullied her into a more confident frame of mind, persuading her to abandon the flat heels, short cropped hair and baggy clothes that Sophie imagined concealed her size, urging her to go to evening classes to learn French and German, and generally encouraging, criticising and sympathising until the never-to-be-forgotten day when she announced Sophie was ready for her first job interviews.

Now, at twenty-six, with her thick wavy hair coiled neatly into her neck, the carefully chosen simple clothes of excellent cut and her high heels, Sophie had a poise and confidence that she owed almost entirely to Lottie Ritter.

'Let me explain,' Lottie was saying. 'The von Hartogs are recently divorced and the children live with their mother. These three weeks skiing is the only time they can spend with their father. And now, with their nanny sick, their mother is threatening to cancel the holiday.' She looked pleadingly at Sophie. 'And it's in Kitzbühl, where you're booked to go in any case for your own holiday! It could all fit in so well,' she coaxed.

'You don't understand,' said Sophie quietly. 'I'm really exhausted. My year in the desert wasn't easy, and I'm not fit to take on another job till I've had a break.'

Lottie didn't comment.

'Then, in five weeks, I start with the Carringtons,' Sophie went on. 'And we both know that won't be a picnic. A new baby with an older child who's been ill and a mother with high society commitments, a father in the diplomatic service . . .' She paused. 'And I do have to see Hilary. She's been nagging me to go down and I've promised.'

'You could see your sister tomorrow,' suggested Lottie. 'And at least the Carrington job's in London, so you can spend your free time in your own flat.'

Sophie looked at the other woman with some curiosity.

'This is really important to you, isn't it?' she asked.

Lottie blushed faintly. 'I used to know the family. A long time ago—before the war. In another world,' she added softly. 'Yes, it does mean a lot to me, and I'd like to help.'

'Why don't you send Sally Hutton? She speaks German.'

'She doesn't ski.'

'You don't have to ski to take kids to ski school.'

'It's more than that. I can trust you with the children. You won't run down the other nanny and split their loyalties.'

Lottie looked rather intently at Sophie. 'You're the best I have and I want them to have you,' she finished roughly.

Sophie's eyes widened in surprise, words trembling on her lips.

'And if you ever dare quote that back to me, I'll deny it,' Lottie added fiercely. 'Every word.'

In the silence the older woman looked almost defiant as Sophie stared at her. Suddenly Sophie smiled. Her mouth curved, her eyes twinkled and her whole face lit up with mischief.

'Well, well,' she murmured softly. 'That is interesting, isn't it? I wonder ...'

'Now look here, Sophie Carter, if you dare ...'

'It's all right,' Sophie interrupted. 'You win. I'll go.'

With a sigh of pleasure, Sophie settled into the window corner of her first-class compartment. So far, the journey had gone without a hitch.

The crisp, cold air of Munich had filled her lungs as she emerged from the airport and climbed into a taxi to take her to the Hauptbahnhof, the main-line station, where she would catch the early evening train across the Austrian border to Kitzbühl. Having trundled her skis to the luggage van, she found her reserved seat and now looked out eagerly at the busy station.

The lights were coming on, and business was brisk at the small glass kiosks selling everything from newspapers and flowers to hot frankfurters, fresh rolls and mouth-watering cakes. Below the vaulted glass ceiling, the electronic signs announced the far-flung destinations of trains waiting patiently below.

The train was crowded. Heavy boots tramped along the corridors, voices were raised in French and German as travellers found their seats, on the way to the mountains for the weekend skiing. Sophie opened her pigskin dressing case, a present from the Arab family she had just left, and checked she had everything to hand : passport, ticket, seat reservation docket and the von Hartog villa address in case no one came to meet her. She removed her German money to a zipped interior pocket and transferred the Austrian currency to her wallet before closing the case to rest it on the seat beside her, her thoughts returning to the previous day.

Her sister had met her at the station, still resentful that Sophie couldn't spend the night as planned.

'I thought you had a couple of weeks before your holiday,' she complained.

'So did I,' responded Sophie cheerfully, 'but something's come up and I have to sandwich in another job. I leave tomorrow.'

'For the fleshpots of the wealthy as usual, I suppose,' Hilary commented acidly as she man-oeuvred the car out of the station forecourt on to the main road to Virginia Water.

'Are the children home?' asked Sophie lightly, determined to steer the conversation into safer channels.

'No, thank God! I've managed to park them for the day. I had the devil's own job getting them to leave once they knew you were coming, and I've had to promise they can come home before you leave.'

'Good—I'm longing to see them. It's been over a year. They must have changed out of all recognition.'

A few moments later they turned into the gravel driveway of the Burton home. Fronted by a modern Georgian façade, it stood in its own grounds surrounded by a belt of cedar trees, which gave it privacy and an impressive aura of affluence. One of several houses built in the same style, its shaved lawns, clipped hedges and brass-studded front doors varied in shape only to distinguish them from each other.

Inside everything was immaculate, with hot-house flowers in tall vases and wall-to-wall carpeting. The central heating enveloped them in instant warmth, the silent hush of the house almost oppresive.

'Drink?' asked Hilary.

'Not for me, thanks, but I'd love some coffee.'

Hilary stopped in mid-stride on her way to the sitting-room.

'Don't worry,' Sophie added quickly. I'll get it. Come and join me in the kitchen.'

As always, the large kitchen was spotless. Labour-saving machines stood ranged along the units, and Sophie plugged in the percolator as Hilary arrived with her drink.

'Anything wrong, Hil?' Sophie asked.

'Just the usual.' Hilary sat down at the centre table.

'Things getting you down?' Sophie prompted.

The ice cubes tinkled as Hilary lifted her tumbler and drank deeply.

'Oh, what's the use of talking about it? You never understand how I feel.'

Sophie didn't comment, sitting down opposite her sister.

'You're so damned cheerful all the time,' Hilary went on. 'It's enough to drive a saint mad!'

'You asked me to come,' said Sophie quietly. 'I thought you wanted to talk.'

'I know I did, but I forget that you can't understand normal people with normal lives. You have this glamorous existence living in fantastic houses all over the world, waited on by servants; you have no idea what a drudgery it is down here, every day like the one before—boring, dull!'

Sophie looked at her sister—the smooth, youthful face, pale gold hair swept back into a sophisticated mass of curls and the slim, petite figure in its expensive Jaeger suit. Was it true? Was she unable to appreciate the problems of her sister's life? Married at seventeen to a succfessful man considerably older, now at twenty-three with two young daughters, Hilary was still a very young woman with no experience except marriage.

'What's wrong—especially—at the moment?' she asked.

Hilary looked down into her glass. 'I'm thinking of leaving Robert and letting him keep the kids.'

Sophie got up and switched off the coffee machine, her back to her sister.

'Is there someone else?' she asked lightly.

'There is another man,' said Hilary flatly, 'but he has no intention of leaving his wife.'

'Does Robert know?'

'I think he guesses. It's not the first time.' She hesitated. 'The trouble is, I don't want to go to bed with Robert any more.'

Sophie picked up her mug and sat down. She didn't comment. Since she herself had never been married, she was hardly qualified to dish out advice, nor would

Hilary welcome her opinion. They were still so different in their personalities and their expectations of life that there was little she could offer that her sister would find acceptable. She wondered why Hilary was confiding in her.

'Robert's sleeping in the spare room,' Hilary went on, 'and I know he won't put up with that for long. He's changed,' she added reflectively. 'He's got quite hard—bossy, too. And he flares up at the least little thing.' She looked at Sophie. 'He can be quite unpleasant.'

'Most men can, I believe, when their wives have affairs with other people,' replied Sophie drily.

'Oh, for God's sake don't be such a prude!' Hilary snapped impatiently. 'All that went out with the dodo! Everybody does it now. Especially down here. Wife swapping's the number one hobby.' She laughed. 'You'd be shocked rigid at the things that go on.' Her lips tightened. 'I bet you wouldn't be so strait-laced if some gorgeous hunk of a man was bent on getting you to bed. It's only frustration that makes women like you prim and proper. I suppose you're still a virgin,' she added contemptuously.

Sophie looked at her sister, her eyes blank, her face controlled. She had grown up with Hilary's taunts and was hardened to them. That she still had the power to wound her Sophie refused to admit, relieved at least that she no longer blushed and stammered when Hilary chose to rile her.

'Don't let's quarrel,' she said after a moment, her voice expressionless. 'Why did you want to see me today? Was it to tell me all this?'

Hilary fiddled with the rings on her left hand, the large sapphire glinting in the weak morning sun filtering through the net curtains. 'I thought perhaps—if I leave Robert—you could help me get a job.'

'Doing what?'

'I'd like to travel, meet new people, get a whiff of the high life, and I thought—well—nannying. I could give it a try. It can't be all that difficult, and I've plenty of experience of children.'

'I see.' Sophie wondered briefly if Hilary was serious or if this was another whim arising out of her mood of despondency. Could she be seriously intending to dissolve her marriage and make her way alone?

'I could probably help you,' she said now. 'But have you thought what you're giving up? All this?' She gestured with one hand. 'You're used to a large house which you don't clean and where you don't pay the bills. It would be very different if you lived alone.'

'You manage,' Hilary pointed out.

'In my fashion. But what I make couldn't run to a car and Jaeger suits.'

'I don't need a lecture,' said Hilary sharply. 'I need help. So can you help me or not?'

'If you really want to nanny I'd put you on to my agent,' Sophie said quietly, 'and she'd explain about training and prospects. There's the Norland course, which takes several years, and there are shorter courses. Then you do one year probationary work before you qualify. After that you can pick and choose your jobs.'

'Years?' Hilary gasped. 'You have to be joking!'

'It's what I did,' Sophie pointed out. 'But, Hilary, are you sure you want this?' she asked more gently. 'Even if you do land a job abroad eventually, it's not all roses. Employers demand value for money whoever they are ... and however rich. You may have pleasant accommodation, but it's hard work. You spend twenty-four hours a day with children who aren't your own, and you have no rights over them. Anything you believe is best for them can be changed by their parents. You become fond of them, of course, but you have to take care they don't become dependent on your affection because you'll be leaving them eventually.'

She looked down at her sister's horrified expression and smiled faintly. 'And you don't exactly meet fabulous people even if they are in the house, because you never socialise with your employers. Nor do you eat or live with the servants. You're an in-between ... respected if you're good at your job, and sometimes even liked, but always alone.' Sophie got up and walked over to the window. She was almost thinking out loud, and from somewhere the words just came. 'And it's no use fantasising about the male members of the household. If any nanny is foolish enough to have an affair with a member of the family, it's the end of her career. She'll find it hard to get another job, because the nanny is always the one to get the blame.'

She turned to her sister to find Hilary staring at her, wide-eyed and disbelieving.

'Are you making this up to put me off?' she demanded.

Sophie shook her head.

'Then why do you do it?'

Sophie shrugged. 'It suits me and I'm good at it. But I don't kid myself it's easy. Maybe I've earned a bit more than other girls, but it's a round-the-clock job. I can't just knock off at five, cover my typewriter and go home. Then there are gaps between jobs when I don't earn and have to live on my savings, or I could be ill, unable to work. The money soon goes. After five years I've a mortgaged one-bedroom flat to show for it. It's not really the high life is it?'

Slowly and smoothly the train slid out of the station past friends and relatives waving on the platform. Then windows were closed and passengers settled. Sophie looked out at the suburban sprawl of Munich, the twin towers of the Frauenkirche receding into the distance, the brilliant green cupolas shining in the late afternoon sun.

Had she been too hard on her sister yesterday? she wondered. The tensions from their childhood never left them, running like a thread through their adult lives. She always felt guilty and depressed after seeing Hilary. It made no sense and there was no reason for it, but she knew she still carried scars from the childhood they'd shared.

Watching elderly parents adore the vivid prettiness of their younger daughter, Sophie had sensed early in life that she herself was not loved in the same way. Her attempts to please and her longing to be close to her sister had always been rebuffed—lightly, and with that tinkling laugh that Hilary used to charm those round her. By the time Sophie had reached her teens she had accepted that her lack of beauty and charm made it hard for her family to love her. And gradually she had withdrawn from them, determined to make no further attempts to seek their affection or approval. She had succeeded. In the years that followed she had made her own life outside the home, finding at school enough to absorb her energies. Returning each evening, she had willed herself to remain outside the charmed circle of her family, fiercely resolved not to intrude where she felt she wasn't wanted. And slowly, painfully she had learned to look on, watching the happiness she could not share.

So when the bombshell fell on the morning of her eighteenth birthday she was armoured against it.

She was not their daughter, they told her gravely. She had been adopted as a baby when they'd given up all hope of a child of their own. Now that she was adult, they felt she had a right to know.

Strangely she had felt nothing. Once the initial shock had passed, she had not even been surprised. It explained so much, making sense of so many things that had bewildered her in childhood. And she recognised their great kindness to her. But for her adoptive parents, she might have been brought up in an institution without home or family, and she knew how difficult it must have been for them to keep her after Hilary was born.

Three years later their sudden deaths within a week of each other had left Sophie with a strong feeling of responsibility for Hilary, and she had hoped the loss might bring them closer together. But it had not happened, and the undercurrents of hostility remained. Was it her fault? Sophie wondered. Did she still envy Hilary her beauty and good fortune—a husband who adored her, a beautiful home and children? She didn't think so. And lately she had sensed that all Hilary's advantages had not brought her the happiness she wanted. But still she wondered if somehow she had failed her sister.

The loud clanging of the handbell brought Sophie out of her reverie as the white-coated waiter appeared to announce the first dinner sitting. Sophie didn't want a meal, and settled for a crisp ham roll and coffee from the trolley that stopped at each compartment.

She felt suddenly tired. The last two days in England had passed in a whirl of activity, the details of packing and preparation giving her little time to rest. She looked at her serviceable watch with its wide leather strap. It would be totally dark by the time she reached Kitzbühl. Finishing her coffee, she leaned back and closed her eyes, not knowing what might await her on arrival at the von Hartog villa.

She woke abruptly as the conductor announced Kitzbühl to be the next stop.

Outside it was pitch dark, and the white blanket of snow lay thick and silent, sweeping up to the mountain peaks now in darkness. Lights twinkled from small villages perched high on the steep slopes and from isolated farms dotted here and there in the muffled landscape.

The air was clear and icy as she slithered in her suede boots down the narrow steps of the train on to the platform, dragging her suitcase behind her. All round her were crowds of people calling to each other, laughing and arguing as they made their way to the trolley where the luggage was being unloaded. Sophie hung back and waited.

As the train slid quietly away from the station, a young man wandered along the platform towards her. Slight and slim, he wore the usual skiing gear of trousers, ski boots and hooded anorak. His face she couldn't see in the dim lights from the station buildings.

'Miss Carter?' He stopped.

'Hello,' she said and held out her hand.

'*Grüss Gott*,' he responded, and they shook hands before he picked up her case. 'My name is Peter Kroner. My sister and I look after the Villa Hartog.'

'I'm grateful you came to meet me,' she said as they made their way to the exit. 'Oh, my skis!' she remembered.

'You have your own?' he asked in surprise.

'Yes.' She turned back. 'They were in the luggage van.'

'Wait here. I'll get them.' A flashlight flickered on in his hand.

Minutes later, having stowed her luggage, Peter Kroner handed her into a luxurious sleigh waiting in the station forecourt. He removed the blankets from the back of the two horses, their breath steaming in the cold night air, and Sophie curled up under the thick fur rug as he jumped into the driver's seat and they were off.

The snow lay banked on both sides of the road, muffling the normal sounds of the night. And the silence was intensified by the tiny bells tinkling lightly on the harness of the horses as they clipped along, the rhythmic hiss of the sleigh the only other sound as they swept through the crisp snow towards the lights of Kitzbühl.

'Lisl, we're here!' Peter Kroner opened the front door of the villa and ushered Sophie into the warmth of the hall just as a sturdy figure emerged from the back of the house. 'My sister,' he introduced.

'Welcome,' said a young voice.

'How do you do?' Sophie smiled and held out her hand to the young girl. About eighteen, with a round face, she wore her blonde hair braided round her head, accentuating the widely smiling blue eyes. She was formally dressed in the Austrian dirndl, the dark skirt, white blouse and close-fitting black knitted waistcoat with its thread of green and silver buttons, the traditional costume still worn by many Austrian women.

'Please take up the suitcase before you put the horses away,' Lisl instructed her brother, and Sophie wondered who was the older of the two. 'I have a meal for you,' she went on, 'but perhaps you wish first for your room?' she enquired quaintly.

'That would be lovely,' Sophie said thankfully, and followed the young girl upstairs. The hall was panelled in warm pine, and two wooden chests flanked the brilliantly coloured ceramic stove that sent the heat rising to the upper floor. At the top of the stairs they turned into a corridor.

'This is the children's wing,' Lisl explained.

'Are they asleep?' asked Sophie in a whisper.

'No,' Lisl laughed. 'They come tomorrow.'

She opened a door at the far end of the corridor just as Peter arrived with her suitcase. That it was lovely was Sophie's first thought. Cosy and light with a comfortable armchair, an open fireplace—an unusual luxury—and a square wooden table with two upright chairs.

'Your bedroom is there,' Lisl pointed, 'the bathroom here. That door leads to the children's rooms and the kitchen.' She turned to Sophie. 'I think you are tired, yes?' she asked. 'So I leave you to unpack. I bring food in half an hour.'

'Wonderful!'

The bedroom was small and simple with its mahogany wardrobe fronted by the traditional bevelled mirror and an enormous bed. Sophie sighed rapturously. So often the beds on offer were too short for her. The long, wide four-poster was the biggest plus of the job so far. Hurriedly she unpacked.

Lying in the bath, which was also long enough for

her to stretch her legs, she thought back to the early jobs of her career with their often cramped accommodation, and the intense loneliness with which she couldn't cope.

'You need a hobby,' Lottie had advised. 'It has to be something you enjoy and can do alone.'

And eventually she had found it. She had always been good at needlework, making many of her nieces' clothes when they were little. And she hit on the idea of sewing her own underwear, finding it made her feel good to know that under the impersonal starch of her outer clothes she was wearing silk cami-knickers, hand-stitched lace and satin bras, and that her nightdress was edged with real lace.

She heard the quiet knock on her living-room door just as she was buttoning her white satin pyjamas. Slipping into high-heeled mules, she pulled on her quilted housecoat, her most ambitious effort to date.

'I do not bring a large meal,' Lisl explained. 'I think it is too late for heavy food. So I have soup, cheese and fruit. It is good, yes?'

'Perfect.' Sophie sat down, the delicious smell of the thick vegetable soup permeating the room.

'Good.' Lisl made to leave. 'Tomorrow after the *Frühstück*—how do you say?'

'Breakfast.'

'*Ach*—you speak my language?'

'A little.'

'I am sad.' Lisl looked disappointed. 'I wish to make my English more good.'

'Then we'll speak English.'

'Thank you. So, tomorrow after—er—breakfast, I take you round, show you all.'

'Excellent, thank you. Oh, Lisl, my skis. Where are they?'

'You have your own? You must ski very good. Downstairs by the house, I expect—with the family skis.'

An hour later, Sophie was more than ready for bed. Taking off her dressing gown, she lay down in front of the fire. However tired she was, she tried to stick to her physical routine. Living at the slow rate of the life of her small charges, she often did not get the exercise she needed, and had worked out a routine of some basic old-fashioned exercises.

Breathing deeply, arms above her head, she stretched, her body responding automatically to the familiar movements. Tipping her weight to her shoulders, her hands on her waist, she lifted her legs and began to cycle in the air.

Suddenly the silence of the house was disturbed. Rapid footsteps pounded along the corridor and without warning her door was flung open.

Sophie turned her head. In the doorway stood the tallest man she had ever seen. Towering above her, he filled the room, and for a moment both figures froze, surprise holding them motionless.

Then a fleeting smile tugged at Sophie's mouth as she realised her ridiculous position with her legs in the air. In one swift movement she brought them down and was on her feet. The man had not moved, and she looked up at him. She was not used to looking up at anyone, but she had a long way to raise her eyes, and so slid into her mules to gain the extra inches. But still she had to crane her neck to find his face.

And then shock blocked her throat. It was the most devastatingly handsome face she had ever seen. Thick, dark russet hair topped a broad forehead with a strong nose. Straight brows stretched across vivid green eyes, and a beautifully moulded mouth was set above a firmly rounded chin. She could see little else of him because he was dressed in a fur-lined leather coat that reached down to high black boots. In his arms he carried several packages, gift-wrapped in different colours.

Finally she found her voice.

'Please close the door behind you,' she asked in German, surprised to hear a husky note in her voice.

But still he stood there. Only his eyes moved. His gaze till now riveted to her face, dropped to her body where the white satin of her pyjamas clung to the contours of her figure.

Sophie felt a blush rise from her neck. No one ever saw her in the silks and satins she wore next to her skin, and she was aware of a strange embarrassment under the intent scrutiny. Awkwardly she reached for her dressing gown. As she slid her arms into the sleeves, his gaze moved to her breasts, their shape clearly visible as her arm movements tightened the thin material across her body.

His lips curled faintly, and his glance continued downward to the curve of her waist, the soft roundness of her hips and the length of her legs. Even that wasn't the end of his appraisal. Slowly, leisurely, his eyes travelled back up her body till they returned to her face, and remained intent on her mouth before he looked into her eyes and noted the flash of anger.

Her embarrassment was fading fast at the presumption of his continued presence in her room. He was obviously used to women falling in a swoon at his feet! Well she was too old for that sort of nonsense, she told herself rather forcefully. As if he could read her thoughts, he suddenly smiled, a genuine smile of amusement that gave a glimpse of white teeth. Sophie caught her breath. Dear heavens—he had charm! No wonder his eyes radiated sexual confidence, the certainty that no woman could resist him.

She had never liked handsome men. They were usually humourless and generally suffered from boundless vanity. And this was obviously no exception. Veiling her eyes with long lashes, she looked up into that smiling face with its practised charm hard at work and wondered how much longer he was going to stand there ogling her.

Finally he pulled himself together. A slight inclination of the head, an abrupt turn and he was gone, closing the door quietly behind him.

To her own amazement Sophie found she was trembling, her legs oddly weak. She must be more angry than she'd realised, she told herself firmly.

Who was he? she wondered. Could he be the children's father? It seemed likely, in view of the parcels he was carrying. But then he would have known she had arrived, and would hardly charge into her room as he had done.

None of it was really important. And none of it explained the oddly strong beat of her heart or her heightened colour as she looked into the mirror in the bedroom. Her skin, too, was tingling with some kind of reaction. Surely she couldn't have been afraid? She had handled more than one nocturnal visitor to her bedroom in her years as a nanny, and none had even faintly raised her pulse rate. It must have been the suddenness of it all, she decided finally before she turned out the light and went to sleep.

CHAPTER TWO

SOPHIE stood at the top of the highest run on the Hahnenkamm. Her alarm clock had woken her at six and she had hurried into her white zipped ski suit and tiptoed downstairs to the vestibule, where she had clipped on her boots and found her skis.

She had been the only one taking the lift at that hour, going from the first to the second stop and on to make her descent from the top. As she was carried slowly and silently high above the sleeping town, the sun had thrown its first rays through the clouds. Now, looking down at the *piste* below her, she could feel the beginning of warmth against her face. One or two people were arriving at the lower slopes, but up here she was quite alone, and a sense of exhilaration touched her, the familiar excitement bringing a tension to her body with the longing to go.

Pulling her goggles down to sit snugly across her eyes, she lifted her sticks and planted them into the compact snow as she slid to the edge of the rise. There had been no fresh snowfall during the night, and the surface of the snow gleamed hard and cold as the sun began to climb. She would have to be careful and remember that this was her first time on skis since the previous spring.

And then she was off, the wind in her face, the snow lying round her as far as the eye could see, and not a soul in sight. Faster and faster she went, taking care, getting the feel of her skis, her body attuning itself to the rhythm of what she loved doing more than anything else. Below her the hollow bit deep into the mountain, and she skirted it carefully where in a few days time she would jump.

As she slowed, a skier whipped past her at tremendous speed and waved his stick in a casual salute. Tall and dressed in black, with the extra-long skis of the expert, he was travelling at a dazzling pace, and she stopped for a moment to watch him as he disappeared from sight into a belt of trees far below, before making her way back to the house.

Lisl caught her as she was climbing the stairs in her stockinged feet.

'*Guten Morgen*,' she said, smiling widely. 'You have been skiing, yes?'

Sophie nodded.

'The Herr Baron has asked for you,' she went on. 'He wishes you to join him for breakfast.'

'At what time?'

'*Neun Uhr*. Come down and I show you,' explained Lisle before they parted.

In her room Sophie stripped and stepped under the shower, and twenty minutes later she was ready. Looking at herself in the mirror, she wondered if the children's regular nanny wore a uniform or the casual jeans that so many younger nannies now adopted. The Norland brown Sophie wore only when going out with her charges. For her indoor duties she had made herself a series of white cotton tunic dresses, worn with a cap into which she could tuck her hair, adding white stockings and medium-heeled serviceable shoes. The whole effect was more that of a nurse than a nanny, and she found children related easily to the image she projected, her place in the household immediately being clear. Over the years she had learned that how she saw herself was very much how she was accepted. The families with whom she worked never questioned the cool, calm efficiency her outward appearance suggested, and for this she was thankful. It enabled her to live as she wished, on the fringe of their lives, looking on. That was safe and familiar territory which she could handle with ease. No one made demands on her that she couldn't meet and she was never involved with the adults and children with whom she lived. And when it was time to move on she could do so without regrets.

If sometimes she wondered what had happened to the passions and despairs of her childhood, she assumed they had faded with time, and felt no urge to resurrect them.

She could barely remember the dreamy teenager who had sat by the hour weaving fantasies of a Sophie very different from the reality, a girl of beauty and allure who could demand and receive admiration and affection, love and passion.

Wryly Sophie smiled into the mirror at the image of the real Sophie—cool, neat, tidy and controlled—light years away from the figment of her youthful imagination.

When occasionally the nightmares returned, erupting with savage violence to remind her that the powerful emotions of her adolescence might still lurk below the outward calm, threatening to destroy her peaceful existence, then she panicked quite horribly. But not for long. The cold light of day banished such terrors, and they were becoming increasingly rare as the years passed and the even tenor of her life remained unruffled.

Her rubber soles made no noise in the quiet of the house as she went downstairs and followed the sound of Lisl's voice to find the kitchen.

'*Gut*,' Lisl greeted her, wiping her hands and taking off her apron. 'Come, I show you.'

The small breakfast room was charming. Dark beams held up a low ceiling, and several windows along one wall let in the brilliant sunlight reflecting the white thick snow that buried the garden outside. Touches of pale yellow in curtains and cushions brightened the room, the ceramic stove in shiny blue, the floor underfoot the same parquet as the rest of the house. In the window recess a round table was set for breakfast.

'I bring coffee,' said Lisl, and disappeared.

Sophie wandered to the windows, her hands in the pockets of her dress. She was aware of an unfamiliar feeling of tension. She disliked waiting. She enjoyed her work, but she was used to organising her own time, eating either alone or with children. She had no wish to eat with her employer, and felt uneasy as she looked down at the table set for two.

'Miss Carter,' a deep voice said behind her in faultless English. At last, she thought, and turned to face the man from last night.

'Maximilian von Hartog,' he said formally.

'Good morning,' she responded politely as he came towards her, hand outstretched.

They shook hands, and she felt the smooth skin of slim fingers and a muscular hand, the grasp firm before he released her and stepped away.

'Won't you sit down?' He gestured to the table.

She nodded and they sat down opposite each other.

'I must apologise for last night,' he said smoothly. 'I'd forgotten you would have arrived, and was looking for somewhere to leave the children's presents.'

'That's all right,' she replied with slight awkwardness. She raised her head to look into his face, aware of a curious dryness in her throat and a slightly nervous tremor. He returned her gaze, cool, formal and polite, the green eyes steady in the tanned face.

Just then Lisl arrived with coffee, rolls, hot milk and curled pats of butter. Fresh fruit and home-made preserves were already on the table.

Sophie relaxed, chiding herself for her nervous qualms as he poured coffee for them both.

'You had a good journey?' he enquired.

'Thank you, yes.'

'I understand you know Kitzbühl. You've been here before?'

'I've spent some holidays here,' she explained easily as she began to eat.

'And you speak German?'

'A little.'

'We are lucky to have you,' he said next. 'Indeed, we're grateful you've come at all. I understand from your agent it was at some inconvenience. You had to re-arrange your plans.'

She didn't respond to that, picking up her cup and drinking the excellent coffee, her attention fully on her breakfast.

'When are the children arriving?' she asked.

'They'll be here in time for lunch. I've arranged with Lisl that she spends time with you this morning showing you the house.'

'Thank you. Can you tell me something of the children's routine while they're here?'

'That was my intention in asking you to join me this morning,' he said drily, and she was aware of a sudden dislike for this cool, handsome man. Did he think she assumed he had a personal interest in having breakfast with her? She raised her chin at the thought and met his eyes. They held a curious smile, almost as though he knew what she was thinking, and she veiled her own expression, waiting for him to continue.

'You will want to deal with their breakfast,' he suggested, quite correctly, 'and your kitchen upstairs is equipped for that. Lisl will arrange for fresh rolls and whatever else you need to be taken up to you each morning.' He paused and bit into a crisp roll, white teeth flashing for a moment in the tanned face. Sophie looked down at her coffee. 'They'll go to ski school in the morning from nine to twelve, I think. You might check the finishing time with the instructor when you take them tomorrow. Lunch they'll have downstairs, and, apart from breakfast, Lisl will make their meals.'

She looked up in surprise, a question on her lips. He gestured vaguely with one well-shaped hand. 'It's easier that way. They're on holiday, and you may wish to go to the ski school yourself while waiting for them. I prefer you to spend time with the children rather than in the kitchen. If you can cope with their personal laundry while they rest, that would be much appreciated by Lisl. She has her hands full at this time of year. We have open house, and different members of the family may drop in for the odd day's skiing. Their evening meal the children will have upstairs, and I leave you to make your arrangements with Lisl, whether you share this with them or eat afterwards.'

He looked across at her.

'There will be days when I wish you to have dinner downstairs because that may be the only time to discuss problems.'

Sophie didn't comment or agree, and after a moment he leaned back, touching his napkin to his mouth, before taking a small cigar and lighting it slowly. His movements were oddly graceful, she thought absently, and she noticed his hands, slim, but strong. In spite of his size, he seemed to carry no fat, his shoulders and arms in the light sweater muscled and powerful.

'That leaves your free time,' he said next.

'I understand I will have one day a week,' she said, her eyes on her plate.

'Will Sunday be suitable?'

'Thank you.'

'And the evenings, of course. If you wish to go out, just let Lisl know and she'll keep an ear open for the children. They're not babies, but if they know you're going out, they may get into mischief.'

'Emil is eleven, I understand, and Erika nine?'

'Yes.' He looked surprised.

'Unfortunately that's the extent of my information. There wasn't time to find out anything else.' She smiled at him, her eyes briefly lit with warmth.

His face suddenly stilled, the cigar in his hand arrested in mid air, the green eyes intent, and Sophie was aware of tension, electrically charged. Her smile died abruptly. The sensation lasted only an instant before he collected himself and got up.

'I believe that's all,' he said. 'Have you any questions?'

'No,' she replied quietly, 'unless there's anything more I should know, any special circumstances that might affect my dealing with the children.'

He was standing by the windows looking out and she had a long way to look up at his profile. His height she had noticed the previous evening, but now she noted the wide shoulders and immensely long legs before he spoke.

'They are children of recently divorced parents, and this I believe you know. But I don't approve of children being handled with kid gloves because they've suffered traumas which should not be part of childhood. On the contrary, the more normal their everyday life, the sooner they'll adapt to changed family circumstances.'

He turned to her.

'I trust to your good sense in dealing with them. I understand from your agent that she chose you because of your sensitivity and understanding.'

Sophie looked back at him with some curiosity. His voice was casual and impersonal. Was he hiding some deeper emotion in talking of his children and the loss of their mother? Her eyes moved to the window. How had the break-up of the family come about? Had his wife left him? Or had he found someone he preferred to the mother of his children? Whatever the traumas he mentioned, his own attitude seemed oddly remote and unfeeling.

Her glance moved back to him to meet an intent stare strangely charged with feeling, almost as though he was demanding something of her that he couldn't put into words. Was he worried that she might hurt his children? Did he think she would be uncaring of their feelings?

She held his gaze, her regard steady, her eyes untroubled.

'I will do my best to ensure they enjoy their holiday without additional tensions,' she said quietly, and relaxed as he withdrew his eyes from their concentrated perusal of her face.

'Thank you,' he said coolly.

'If you'll excuse me now,' she said, and got up. He didn't turn as she walked quietly out of the room.

It was mid-morning when the quiet of the house

erupted into noise. Sophie heard the tramping of feet mingle with the low murmur of voices and guessed that the children had arrived. Casting a last look round the nursery to check everything was neat and tidy, she walked out on to the landing. Through the windows she could see the sleigh drawn up outside, the children climbing down as Peter unstrapped the luggage. Slowly she made her way downstairs.

She was half-way down when the front door opened. At the same moment, Maximilian von Hartog came out into the hall from his study. So he had not fetched the children from the station, she thought fleetingly before the two youngsters came charging into the hall below her.

'*Onkel Max. Onkel Max*!' The little girl ran across and hurled herself into his arms. Uncle Max. So he was not the children's father, he was their uncle. She looked down at him in total astonishment as he bent to scoop up the child who wound her arms tightly round his neck and kissed him passionately on both cheeks.

'Hello, little one,' he greeted her, and lifted his head to glance up at Sophie, his eyebrows raised in ironic amusement. Sharply she turned away. He had done it deliberately, she thought, misleading her at breakfast, and she felt a spurt of anger at his arrogance before her attention was drawn away from him.

Coming towards her now was another man. Tall, slightly stooped and thin, he was dressed in a thick overcoat and fur hat. Brown eyes regarded her steadily as he pulled off his gloves and smiled gently.

'Miss Carter?' he asked in a soft voice, and held out his hand. 'Klaus von Hartog, the children's father.'

Sophie walked down the remaining steps and took the outstretched hand.

'Welcome,' he said in German. 'I trust you've been made quite comfortable.'

'Thank you, yes.'

'May I present my son, Emil?' he introduced the boy, drawing him forward. 'Make your bow to Miss Carter, Emil,' he instructed. The boy took Sophie's hand and clicked his heels, bowing his head briefly before he lifted serious eyes to stare up at her. Thin and slight with soft blond hair brushed neatly back from an intelligent forehead, he had a small, rather anxious face.

'Emil,' acknowledged Sophie gravely.

'And my daughter Erika.' He turned to his daughter. 'Nanny Carter,' he said to her.

Still held by her uncle, she looked down into Sophie's face.

'Erika,' Sophie said quietly as she met the fierce look of the little girl. Very pretty, with softly rounded cheeks and the same blue eyes as her brother, she had thick blonde hair worn in two plaits down her back.

'You're not my nanny,' she said crossly.

'No, I'm not,' said Sophie quietly before either of the men could speak.

'I'm not going to call you nanny,' the child continued with a heavy frown. Her uncle lowered her to the ground and Sophie looked down at her.

'What will you call me, then?' she asked softly.

'Nothing. I don't like you and I won't speak to you at all.'

'That's enough, Erika!' her father said sharply. 'You will apologise to Miss Carter for your rudeness. At once, please.'

'No, I won't, Papa.' The small face set rebelliously and Sophie intervened.

'I wonder how we'll manage if you don't speak to

me?' she asked reflectively. 'Perhaps you could use sign language.'

'That's silly,' said Erika loftily. 'I don't know any sign language. Anyway, you wouldn't understand.'

'True,' Sophie said thoughtfully. 'Well, I'm sure we'll think of something. But now it's time to unpack and change. And for that I'll need your help to show me where everything belongs.'

Sophie didn't take her eyes off the little girl, the tension between herself and her charge clearly evident in the silence round them. 'There are some surprises upstairs to be unpacked,' she went on, and turned casually towards the stairs. 'And, of course, Nanny's get well card to write.'

'What's a get well card?' asked Erika curiously, quite forgetting her resolve.

'I'll show you,' Sophie answered calmly, and started up the stairs. 'Come along Emil,' she added without turning round.

Below her no one moved. But she continued up the stairs at a slow, even pace.

'Right. See you at lunch, then,' said Maximilian von Hartog lightly. 'A drink, Klaus?' He turned to the other man, and suddenly the oddly tense tableau came to life. Peter picked up the cases and headed for the stairs in Sophie's wake, Emil muttered something inaudible and followed, and Klaus von Hartog shed his coat, then the two men walked into the study, leaving Erika alone in the hall.

Still Sophie didn't check or look back. Above her she heard Emil give a shout.

'Wow!' came his voice, and it was finally too much for the little girl. She clambered up the steep stairs and ran past Sophie.

'Wait for me, Emil,' she cried. 'I want to see!'

With a small smile, Sophie followed her along the corridor and into the nursery.

The children were asleep. Sophie left the bedroom door slightly ajar in case one of them woke and made her way to the small kitchen to wash up.

On the whole things had gone well. The unpacking of gifts, the writing of the card to Nanny Elisabeth and lunch with their father and uncle had all helped to break the ice. After lunch Sophie had been firm about a rest, and later they had all walked down into the town where Sophie had treated them to hot chocolate and a sticky cake before they trudged home to baths and a light evening meal. By the time she had read them a story they were almost asleep.

When she had come to wake them after their rest, she had found them both in Emil's bedroom. They had stopped talking abruptly as she walked in, and Emil had coloured vividly; she guessed they had been talking about her. But she was familiar with hostility when she first joined a household and had ignored Erika's attempts to needle her, making no move to ingratiate herself with the children or be severe with them. After supper she had kept them both so busy with carefully planned activities and plans for the days to come that even Erika forgot her anger in the excitement of new games and the physical jerks that Sophie explained they would be doing together each evening.

She hung up the kitchen towel and glanced at her watch. It was time to go down. Earlier, Klaus von Hartog had requested her to come downstairs once the children were in bed, gravely promising that he would not keep her long.

Voices sounded from the sitting-room, and she knocked.

'*Herein.*'

The two men rose as she appeared in the doorway.

'Good evening, Miss Carter. Please come and sit down.' Klaus von Hartog pulled forward an easy chair to face the fire. Maximilian von Hartog nodded politely and left them. Sophie was conscious of relief; he made her feel uneasy.

'Now tell me how the day went,' he asked with friendly interest.

'Quite well, I think.'

'They're both emotional, as I'm sure you noticed, and Erika does have these sudden outbursts. But your calm kindness will soon simmer her down. She is very much like her mother,' he added, a slow flush mounting under his skin. He's still in love with his ex-wife, guessed Sophie.

'This time last year we were all here together, so this is our first holiday without her.'

Suddenly the door opened behind her and Maximilian von Hartog came back. Sophie stiffened.

'Coffee will be here in a moment,' he said, and smiled blandly at them both, sitting down again in the same chair.

'I understand my cousin has told you we don't wish to dwell on family problems while the children are here,' Klaus von Hartog went on.

His cousin! So the two men were not brothers; that explained the startling difference between them: the one so tall and broad, totally masculine, while the other seemed almost frail, perhaps prematurely aged with the break-up of his marriage. There was a sadness in his face, a sense of resignation as though fate had dealt harshly with him. And Sophie sensed he was making no move to fight for what he wanted. She couldn't imagine his cousin permitting the woman he loved to leave him. Maximilian von Hartog would fight ruthlessly to keep her or dismiss her from his life and thoughts without a backward glance. She was not looking at him, but could feel his eyes on her face and wished he would occupy himself with something.

'I want to spend as much time as I can with the children, but there are problems,' the other man was saying. 'I'm a surgeon and there are several operations to which I'm committed, and for these I will have to return to Vienna. The children understand about my work, of course. They're used to it. But in the past they've had their mother to turn to in my absence. This will be the first time she has not been with them.' He coloured again and then cleared his throat. 'I hope you won't find this an additional burden, because it does mean I have to rely on you rather heavily from time to time.'

'I will do my best,' said Sophie quietly, wondering why he had not kept them with him in Vienna.

'My wife—their mother——' he amended, '—and I did not wish to deprive them of their skiing holiday. We felt it best not to disrupt their normal routine.'

'I can appreciate that,' Sophie said easily.

'You're leaving tomorrow, Max?' asked his cousin.

'No.' Maximilian von Hartog was looking a Sophie again. 'I'll be staying on for a while.'

'That's marvellous.' The older man's brow cleared. 'The children adore their uncle, Miss Carter, especially Erika. And he can always cope with them if things get difficult.'

'I, too, will do my best,' drawled Max von Hartog.

Sophie sat up straight in an effort to throw off the strange effect he was having on her. Even without looking at him, she was aware of the relaxed power of his tall figure, the intent stillness of his eyes on her face. Carefully she shut him out of her consciousness and concentrated on the children's father.

'Anyhow I want to be here as much as possible.' Dr von Hartog grinned rather endearingly, and Sophie chided herself for feeling contempt for his apathy. It was obvious that he was a surgeon of considerable repute, and Sophie was well aware that talented and successful people did not always have the ability to find happiness in their personal relationships.

'I'll take them to ski school in the morning and bring them back to lunch. Then I'll hand them over to you for a few hours and come up in the evening to sit with them while they eat. Is that convenient?'

'Of course,' she responded warmly. 'I'll organise each day as it fits in with your free time.'

'Thank you.' He smiled ruefully. 'I was a little afraid you might wish to have a strict routine.'

'I'll be taking them out tomorrow afternoon, Miss Carter,' Max von Hartog intervened.

Sophie nodded without looking at him. 'Perhaps you'll give them time for a short rest after lunch,' she said quietly.

'Of course. Just bring them down when they're ready. I'll be taking them up to the top of the Hahnenkamm by cable car, and I'll expect you to join us, if you please.'

Sophie stiffened. 'I would rather use the time for some chores, if you don't mind.'

'That will have to wait. It's important they see us together. They have to understand that we trust you. Then, when you're alone with them at a later date, there'll be a clear link with the family.'

Sophie knew she couldn't object. Much as she

would dislike an afternoon spent in his company, he was quite right. If she was seen to be on good terms with their uncle, the children would find it easier to trust her. She looked back at the older man.

'Is there anything else?' she asked politely.

'No.' The Herr Doktor rose courteously. 'Unless you'd like to join us for coffee? But then you haven't yet eaten, I believe,' he corrected himself, 'and you must be pretty tired.'

Maximilian von Hartog rose to open the door for her and she slipped out into the hall with a quiet goodnight. A moment later she found him beside her.

'Just a minute.'

Unwillingly she stopped at the bottom of the stairs.

'Will you give me the pleasure of dining with me tomorrow night?' he asked softly. She looked at him in astonishment. 'Not here,' he added quietly. 'Out somewhere.'

She dropped her eyes and looked past him at a singularly uninteresting portrait on the wall behind him. 'Thank you, no. I'm afraid that's not possible.'

'Have you another engagement?' he demanded.

Devoutly she wished she had. 'No,' she said baldly.

She could feel his smile on her face, almost indulgent, as though he was amused by her refusal.

'I don't socialise with my employers,' she added.

'Why ever not?' He sounded genuinely surprised.

'I don't believe I owe you any explanations about my private life, Herr Baron.' Sophie heard the prim note in her voice and was fleetingly angry with herself.

'You use my title to keep me at a distance?' he asked lightly. 'But you see, I never use it. It's outdated and has no place in the modern world.'

At that she did look at him, surprised by the hint of

steel in his voice. Had she misjudged him? He was still smiling, his eyes teasing her, but she sensed there was more to the man than his indolent manner suggested.

'Please excuse me now,' she said politely, and made to go past him up the stairs.

'You haven't answered my question,' he pointed out, and barred her way, one hand gripping the banisters.

She felt breathless, hemmed in between his outstretched arm and his body that was suddenly much too close.

'Well?'

'My answer is still the same,' she said quietly, her head turned away from him.

'But what of your own wishes . . . leaving aside the rules for a moment. Would you like to have dinner with me?' He bent his head towards her.

'Thank you, but I don't wish to go out with you,' she said awkwardly, wishing he would move away.

But he didn't stir. Nor was he in the least put out.

'You are lying, my dear Sophie. And you're not very good at it. If you relaxed that iron guard for a moment, you'd know I mean you no harm.'

Angry at his use of her Christian name, she was aware that she felt flustered and suddenly unable to deal with him.

'Please,' she said unsteadily, 'let me go.'

He moved up a step closer to her and she panicked, flinching away from him, her back against the banisters behind her.

'You're taking advantage of me—my position in this house,' she whispered, using a phrase that had worked in the past with other men.

At that his face closed and he stepped back without a word. Hurriedly she brushed past him and almost

ran upstairs, her breathing shallow, her heart
pounding uncomfortably. At the top she stopped and
pulled herself together. Looking back, she saw he
hadn't moved, was standing quite still in the hall, his
face raised to hers.

Rather unsteadily she walked away from him along
the corridor to her room.

CHAPTER THREE

THE outing with Maximilian von Hartog the following afternoon turned out quite differently from what Sophie had secretly feared.

They set off for the cable car station on foot, dressed in boots, trousers and hooded anoraks, the children skipping and jumping at their uncle's side; Sophie was relieved that she could remain in the background as he kept them amused with stories of the intrepid explorers who climbed the Tyrolean glaciers. How much was true and how much dramatised she didn't care to guess. It was all very enjoyable and kept the children alternately breathless with excitement and shrieking with laughter.

The slow journey up in the cable car was dazzling, even Erika reduced to silence by the wonder of the towering mountains ahead and the valley receding below. At the top they had a snowball fight which Emil battled with relentless determination, and it ended with both children burying their uncle in snow, from which he escaped to chase them across to the *Gasthaus* for a break.

Sitting on his lap, Erika flirted shamelessly with him, as though nearer twenty than ten years old, and he responded with old-world gallantry until they were all in fits once more. Finally he allowed the children to play with two boys of their own age whose parents were quite happy to keep an eye on all four, leaving Sophie alone with him in the rapidly emptying café.

They chatted desultorily, neither feeling the need to talk, words flowing easily when they had something to say, the silence, when it came, oddly companionable. Max told her of his visits to London, and they shared memories of parks, art galleries and the opera houses which he knew well. Music was his first love, and as a teenage boy he had longed to be an opera singer. He had studied for several years, but in the end family responsibilities had claimed him. Looking back, he admitted ruefully, he saw that his voice had not really been good enough to build a successful singing career. Sophie talked of her travels the people she met and the countries she had visited.

The shadows lengthened and still they sat on, until finally conversation lapsed. Sophie looked out at the darkening skyline, curiously content, more relaxed with him than she could recall being with anyone. She felt no need to chat politely as she would have done with most strangers.

'Can I now persuade you to have dinner with me one evening?' he asked suddenly, and leaned towards her across the table. She stiffened, and he continued, 'Do you realise how rare it is to find someone with whom communication is so easy?'

'I'm sorry,' she answered him reluctantly. 'I . . .'

'Don't socialise with employers,' he finished for her. 'I know. Nanny code.'

'In a way,' she admitted.

'Not all nannies abide by it,' he drawled mockingly. 'Nanny Lisa is quite prepared to break this particular rule.'

'Then you've only another three weeks to wait for her return,' said Sophie tartly.

'Well, well—claws!' He raised his eyebrows at her. 'I'm delighted. But I have to disillusion you. It's my cousin on whom she wishes to bestow her favours. I've never asked for them.'

Sophie turned her head away as the colour surged into her face. 'I think we should go,' she mumbled, bending her head as she gathered her things.

'In a moment.' He put out a hand and she sank back in her seat. 'Perhaps we could meet when you're no longer with my family?' he suggested quietly.

Sophie swallowed. How could she tell him that nothing would be changed when she left? She was no teenager, and knew full well what he wanted of her. A sudden quiver of feeling trembled through her at the thought of intimacy with Maximilian von Hartog. But she controlled it at once.

She had not had affairs. Her body had developed early, and in her mid-teens several boys had been attracted by her physical maturity, hoping to persuade her to bed. But she had been curiously repelled by their response to the voluptuous curves which only embarrassed her, and she had known even at sixteen this was not for her. Her fellow students at Norland had also tried to explain how much fun it could be, encouraging her to take the plunge. But still she had held back.

Had she been afraid of intimacy with a man because it involved plunging into the unknown, shedding her reserve and permitting another human being to come close to her? Or could Hilary be right that she was a prude? In recent years it had ceased to be a problem, and she rarely thought about it. Perhaps if she ever met a man she wanted passionately, she would change her mind. But he would have to be of her world, not a sophisticated, handsome aristocrat who had doubtless made love to scores of beautiful women and would expect her to be experienced, fully able to treat a casual encounter with light-hearted ease. Maximilian von Hartog was not the man for her—whatever he wanted.

She turned her eyes to his face. He was no longer looking at her, his head in profile, his eyes intent on his own thoughts as he stared out of the window at the landscape rapidly darkening into the cold grey of evening. His hair lay thick and sleek against his head, and she felt a sharp urge to reach out and slide her fingers through its silky length. The tanned skin had a polished sheen and almost she could feel it—faintly rough—under her fingertips.

As she gazed at him a curious pain twisted slowly deep inside her, spiralling outward and bringing a heavy weakness to her limbs. His face began to swim out of focus and she closed her eyes to blot him out of her mind. But his image remained under her lids, vivid and painfully real.

The blood pounded in her head and she began to tremble, dizzy with sensations she couldn't control. Desperately she pressed her knees tightly together and clamped her hands on the arms of her chair, clenching her stomach muscles to fight her way back to sanity.

Slowly the turbulence subsided. Her body stopped shaking, but she felt drained and limp, her face damp with heat, the past few moments unlike anything she had ever experienced. He had done nothing, yet without touching her he had managed to evoke a shattering response in her body, frightening in its intensity. How was it possible, when she had rejected him? How could her body respond against her will, against the dictates of reason?

He was a powerfully attractive man with a mouth and hands that hinted at a strong sensuality. And somehow he had managed to reach through her defences. But it must not happen again. She would have to tread warily, ensure she was never alone with him, and keep her distance at all times. Only a vast experience of women could have given him the undoubted understanding of her sex that she sensed below the surface of his charm, and she would have to arm herself against his attractions.

She sensed he could disrupt her life and throw her into a turmoil from which she might never emerge. If she let him. She clung to that thought. He could harm her only if she let him.

'Please accept my refusal,' she said now without looking at him, her voice low. 'I don't enjoy saying no.'

She heard the quick intake of his breath as his head turned sharply towards her. Seeing the anger in his eyes, she guessed she had wounded his pride.

'I don't give up easily,' he said tautly. 'And whatever you say to me with words, your eyes tell me a different story. So don't imagine this is the end. Whatever it is we share, you and I are just beginning, Sophie Carter.' He stood up. 'Now, shall we find the children?' he added coldly.

Sunday came quite suddenly, and the day stretched ahead to do with as she wished.

As Sophie reached the top of her favourite *piste* the sun was rising, and her toes curled with sudden pleasure inside her boots. She adjusted her goggles and looked round. The fall of snow during the night had been steady and deep, and it now lay in virgin fields to the horizon. She would be making her own trails, the dream of any experienced skier. Putting her head down and bending into her knees, she began the decent.

The silence was magical. Ahead of her the firs on both sides were weighed down with fresh snow, their branches bent low, threatening to crack under the weight. As she increased speed, the wind caught her face, the warmth of the sun caressing her back. A camera could never do it justice, she thought. Picture postcards always looked unreal, as though the snow was iced on to the scenery. But up here, quite alone, with the sun beating down on her bare head, the cold tang of the snow in her nostrils and the heady thinness of the air in her face, it was all too real. And intoxicating. Nowhere else in the world did she feel this freedom, as though her body was weightless, swinging through the snow, at one with the nature all round her.

She was about half-way down when she heard the noise. It sounded like a pistol shot, and she swept into a christiana to stop and look back. But there was no one above her. Everything was still, and she continued.

Later, thinking back, she realised that it was her proximity to the trees that probably saved her. As she swerved to give them a wide berth, she heard the roar behind her. Distant at first, it seemed to gain momentum by the minute, the noise louder by the second, and suddenly she knew she was in the path of an avalanche.

Unlikely with the newly powdered snow, it was gaining on her with enormous speed and power. Looking back, she wondered if she could avoid it by hurling herself sideways into the trees, but they were too far away. Panic-stricken, she branched out, skiing across instead of down its path.

The snow hit her has she bent down to ease the onslaught, arms outstretched. Then she fell and knew nothing more.

She woke to blackness and suffocation. There was no air and she couldn't breathe. She panicked and struck out, only to fall back as more snow fell in on her. Sinking her teeth into her lower lip, she tried to pull herself together. Any hope of survival depended on what she did next.

She knew the drill and tried now to apply it. Forcing down her fear, she took stock.

Shallow, slow breathing. No movement of head or body. She could hear nothing. With luck the avalanche had passed and the snow settled. Cautiously she began to scrape some snow away from her face; slowly and with infinite care she increased the breathing area round her head and made a small dent in the hard-packed snow.

Triumphantly she cleared an inch, then another, gently packing it away from her face. Carefully she let out her pent-up breath. The snow stayed. She had begun to create a tiny cave in which there would be a limited amount of oxygen.

Sophie knew her main enemy was terror. It locked in her throat, tore at her nerves and pumped her heart at a frightening rate—the certainty that she would die of suffocation. She had to find something to think about, to still the dread and to calm her breathing, The heat of the packed snow and the cold of her body were wreaking havoc in her brain. And she had no wish to sink into delirium.

She wondered if she had broken anything, if her skis had gone, the bindings having broken loose on impact. She couldn't feel her lower body, and didn't try to move. Did anyone know she was up here? she thought next. Only the man at the ski lift who had clipped her ticket. Would he remember her? Had he heard the avalanche? And would they bother to send help if he remembered that she had gone up?

Her breathing was too fast. She could feel her heartbeat accelerate. She had to slow down. Closing her eyes, she tried desperately to relax.

She must have dozed, for she woke to a noise. Could it be? It sounded like a voice ... calling. But it was muffled, as though reaching her through cotton wool. Unthinkingly she sat up with sudden hope. This time the fall of snow was heavy, entering her mouth, blocking her face. Pulling in her breath, she began again scooping, little by little creating again a tiny space in which to breathe.

'Sophie, can you hear me?'

It was Max.

For a moment sheer joy kept her motionless.

'Don't answer me. Don't try to shout.' She could just make out his words echoing faintly from a distance. 'If you can hear me, do as I say.' He sounded quite calm. 'Try and find your hand and see if your stick is still looped round your wrist. I'll give you a moment to do that.'

She looked down at her hand and lifted it carefully, feeling with the fingers of the other hand till she reached her wrist. Amazingly, her stick was still attached to the wrist.

'If it's there,' Max continued, 'pull it up towards you, slowly and carefully. I want you to push it above your head, out of the snow.'

She pulled, but the stick was firmly stuck below her. She couldn't move it.

'I'm going to get you out,' his voice continued reassuringly. 'I know you're here somewhere: I found one of your skis. And I'll stay here and get you out if I have to dig my way through every inch of snow. But to make it quicker, you must try and help me.'

Sophie felt the tears running down her cheeks, relief and hope struggling with the fear inside her.

'If it's stuck, use your hand to make a little tunnel for it. But be careful. Take it slowly.'

It was almost as though he could see what was happening to her, she thought, and she did as he commanded, trying hard not to rush it. Twice she gave up, certain she hadn't the energy to go on, wanting only to lie down and sleep, unable to find the strength to move even a finger.

'Keep trying. Don't give up,' he called urgently, and she wondered if there was some unspoken communication between them, that he knew how weak she felt.

She was certain the web at the bottom of the stick was the cause of her difficulties. It was too hard to dislodge. Suddenly impatient, she heaved at it and felt the stick move upwards in her hand. At the same moment a fall of snow buried her completely, shutting her off from what little air was left. It was up her nose, in her ears and smothering her face. She was finally suffocating . . . unable to breathe . . .

No. She wouldn't give in now, with help so near.

Cautiously she moved her head and blew the snow out of her nose and mouth. By sheer effort of will she didn't breathe in heavily as she longed to do, but closed her mouth and held her breath. And suddenly she knew what Max wanted. She could no longer hear his voice, but she guessed how he planned to find her.

Carefully she pulled the sling over her hand to free the stick. It seemed to take hours, and several times she had to stop and breathe tiny breaths through her nose. But finally it was free and she pushed it slowly above her head. If she could penentrate the blanket of snow covering her, he might be able to see the tip of the stick above the white and know where she was buried. She went on pushing until the steel tip of the base was between her fingers.

Then she fainted.

The next thing she knew was a dazzling light blinding her eyes and the precious feel of oxygen in her face. Dimly she heard Max's voice as he shovelled with his hands to free her body, murmuring words she couldn't understand.

Finally he lifted her out and carried her away. And all the time he was talking she was bemused, only half conscious as he stood her on his skis in front of him and belted her against his body, the only sound being her breath coming in deep, desperate gasps. His arms held her upright as they moved forward slowly.

The going seemed endless, and she was aware of little, the only reality the feel of Max's body supporting her. Slowly the ragged sound of her breathing died. She quietened, feeling the blessed freshness of air in her face. And all the time he was talking to her.

'Easy now. Slowly. It's all right. You're safe. I won't let you fall.'

Gradually her heart slackened its furious beat, although her legs felt like jelly and only his hold on her kept her upright. But she was deeply thankful to be alive.

'Just a little further, my dearest love,' he whispered into her hair. 'We're nearly there.'

Finally he stopped. Bending to free his skis, he picked her up and carried her in somewhere. Putting her down on a hard bed, he covered her with a blanket and unclipped her boots. As he put a match to the fire laid out in the grate, Sophie looked round. They were in a hut. Two camp beds stood against the wooden walls, and opposite, a small cooking stove was set under a shelf holding emergency rations. The fire began to crackle, catching the dry wood, and steam poured from the kettle. Max put a mug with hot bouillon against her lips, and she drank a few drops before her head sank back and she was asleep.

When she woke it was dark. She could see the mountain filling the window, and wondered for a moment where she was. Then she remembered. A huge fire crackled. A paraffin lamp lit the small hut, and Max's shadow loomed large and dark against the wall before she saw him sitting on a chair, his elbows on his knees, motionless, gazing into the fire.

She stirred, moving to get up, and he was instantly at her side.

'You're awake.'

'I must have slept.'

'It was what you needed most.' He put out a hand and stroked her hair from her face. 'I have some food ready. You must eat something and then we'll talk.'

'I'm not hungry.'

'I know,' he said calmly, 'but you must eat. It's nothing exciting—some soup and crackers—but you won't be able to think till you've eaten.'

They ate in silence. Then Max stirred the fire and replenished the logs while Sophie sat at the end of the bed, a blanket wrapped round her. Slowly her mind began to work. Had she dreamed Max's cry to her up on the mountain? Had he called her his dearest love? Or had she imagined it in her fevered state?

She felt weak and light-headed, and tried to

prepare herself for what he would tell her. They were obviously marooned here for the rest of the night, and she thought vaguely of the family. Would they wonder what had happened? Or would they know and send out search parties? And where had Max been when the avalanche had hit her? Had he been up on the mountain? Or had he heard of the snowfall and come for her? Her heart lurched rather painfully at the thought.

'Now,' he said as he took the empty mug from her fingers, 'we'll talk.'

The hot soup was having its effect. Her mind was clearing and her strength returning, at least in part. She lifted her head and looked at him, her face quite calm, without expression.

He looked huge in the small hut. He had taken off his anorak, and the closely fitting skiing trousers hugged the slim hips and long muscular legs, the black sweater emphasising the broad shoulders and wide chest. He sat down, hands clasped loosely between his knees. He looked tired, the lines down his cheeks dark and the vivid green eyes drooping with fatigue as he looked across at her.

'I don't believe there's anything broken,' he said in a low, even voice. 'The doctor will tell us in due course. But you must try to move as little as possible.'

Sophie nodded, keeping her eyes deliberately blank.

'Have you any pain?' he asked next. She shook her head.

'You're in shock and you'll have to keep very quiet for a few days. With luck that'll be the extent of the damage.'

'How——' she began throatily. 'How,' she repeated more clearly, 'did you know ...'

'Where to find you?'

'No.' She shook her head again, trying to think clearly. 'How did you know about the avalanche?'

'I was up there,' he answered flatly.

She looked at him wide-eyed, questioning, but he didn't enlighten her. His lips tightened, and she decided not to question him further. He was too exhausted to cope.

'We'll wait till daylight,' he said slowly, 'then we'll use the sledge to get down.' He turned, indicating the large sledge standing upright against the wall. 'They'll assume we'd try to get here if I found you. Once they see the light they'll know we're safe.'

He looked back at her. 'In a moment I'm going to try and sleep for a while. It's essential, if I'm to get us down, that I'm not too tired.' She nodded. 'But first you must tell me if you're all right.' He looked into her face, frowning slightly in concentration. 'God knows I'd rather spend the time with you,' he said wearily. 'Come.' He got up. 'Try and stand. Then we'll know if anything is hurting.'

He reached down for her hands and pulled her up. In her thick socks she slipped on the wooden floor and fell heavily against him, her hands gripping him tightly to keep upright. He moved his fingers to her arms and made her stand away from him as he peered anxiously into her face.

'You're so pale it's difficult to know what you're feeling. While you were asleep,' he went on grimly, 'there were moments when I wasn't sure if you were breathing, you were so still.'

She smiled at that. 'I'm all right, thank you,' she said quietly. 'Please don't worry about me. You must get some sleep.'

'Very well,' he sighed, and released her, easing her

back on to the bed. Then he moved quietly and lay on the other bed, pulling a blanket over himself. Silently she waited for his easy breathing telling her he was asleep. But it didn't come.

'I think I'm too tired to sleep,' he said, and sat up.

Sophie lay back and turned away from the sight of him, her longing to touch him, to soothe him to sleep almost too strong to resist. Under the heavy blanket she clenched her hands, willing her thoughts to other things, but too vitally aware of him to still the trembling of her body, the fast beating of her heart.

'It's no good,' he said suddenly, and got up, throwing the blanket aside impatiently. 'We have to talk. The words are beating in my brain.'

Sophie didn't move.

'I'm thirty-five years old and I've seen a good deal of the world. I've met my share of women and known some of them intimately. But there's never been anyone like you. I know we're virtually strangers; we've spent almost no time together. But somewhere deep down in my bones I know you, Sophie Carter, almost as though you were part of me, of my flesh and blood as I want you to be.'

Sophie lay still, her back to him, trying to control the trembling of her body.

'And don't hide from me,' he ground out, striding across and pulling the blanket off her hunched body. 'Look at me.'

Carefully she sat up and looked at him as he towered above her, anger spilling through the exhaustion in his face. Slipping past him, she walked unsteadily to the fire, sitting on a small stool and looking into the leaping flames, trying to still the thumping of her heart, to hide from him the response she felt at his words.

Was this love, she wondered suddenly, this yearning for closeness, the acute awareness of every bone and muscle of his body in the confines of the hut? Or was it merely sexual passion, so new to her that she seemed powerless to control it?

'I'm not going to touch you,' he said softly, misunderstanding her movement. 'But don't imagine I can't tell how you feel. 'I've seen your eyelids quiver as you hide your eyes from me. I've watched your mouth tremble as I look at you. And I've felt your regard on my face as I turn away. I'm aware of you in every fibre of my being,' he went on huskily, 'and my longing for you is there every time I close my eyes and see you again as I did that first time—the black hair cascading down your body, the white pyjamas hiding the secrets of your skin and the beauty of your long legs that I ache to feel closing round me as I lie between them.'

'Please ... no.' Sophie put her hands to her face, flushing with the heat of his lovemaking. His words made her senses swim as though he was touching her, as though his hands were caressing her skin and his body was lying against hers.

'Why, Sophie? Why do you deny us what we both want so ardently? Because you do want it, don't you? Tell me you do.'

'Please,' she whispered again, her eyes veering from his face, 'I can't ... I'm feeling so weak ... I don't know what to say.' Her voice broke. 'I'm so thankful—grateful for what you did today. If you hadn't been there ... did what ... I'd be dead. I'll never forget it.'

'Stop it!' Max commanded harshly. 'Do you know what I felt when I heard that avalanche and saw you disappear below me? Have you any idea? If I hadn't known already, it would have stared me in the face at that moment. I was ready to dig you out with my bare hands, to find you if I had to sweep away every inch of fallen snow.'

He got up and stood with his back to her, his head bent to the fire.

'The fear that I might be too late gripped me so hard I couldn't move with the agony of losing you.' His voice was harsh and his breathing ragged. He turned back to her and reached down to grip her arms, pulling her up to face him.

She winced at the hard strength of his fingers, and her eyes swam with tears of weakness.

'Why, Sophie?' he asked again. 'What is it that makes you say no? Are you afraid I might hurt you? Be brutal . . . clumsy?' His voice softened. 'Don't you know I would be gentle and tender, that I'd want you to share every moment of my pleasure?'

'I know,' she whispered, and looked up at him, unable to hide her longing for him. Her eyes fell before the passion in his face, her body trembling with the desire to give him what he wanted.

Only it was all happening too quickly. He was overwhelming her with emotion, and still she wasn't sure what he wanted. Did he expect to make love to her here—tonight—and then leave her tomorrow, walk out of her life? Or did he want an affair with her at the villa while she was working for his family? She didn't know and couldn't bring herself to ask. Miserably she wished she knew more about men.

And she felt so odd. Her head was dizzy with tension and her mind wouldn't function properly. Her lids were so heavy she was finding it hard to keep her eyes open. In shock, Max had said. Could that be what was the matter with her? Abruptly she sat down, hoping she wouldn't faint at his feet.

'Later today I go away,' he said, his face now under control, his voice even. 'I've been here too long and telephones are claiming me. I have to return to my responsibilities.'

Looking down intently into her face, he paused, waiting for her to speak.

'Well?' he asked at last, and the single, quiet word was almost her undoing, more difficult to resist than his passionate outcry of moments earlier. She felt the tears lock in her throat and longed to throw herself into his arms. But her strength had finally deserted her.

'Please,' she whispered, 'I can't ... I'm not up to this just now.'

She raised her face pleadingly to his. For a moment he said nothing, then he seemed to come to a decision.

'And dead on your feet,' he commented finally, and sighed. 'Very well.'

And then he moved, bending to lift her up into his arms and holding hers tight against him.

'Give me your lips, Sophie,' he demanded urgently, 'just once.'

There was nothing she wanted more, and she raised her face. His mouth was a revelation. Never had she imagined such passion and tenderness, demanding and giving until her head swam. And she kissed him back, passionately, opening her mouth to his, responding wildly, urging her body closer to the hard warmth of his. Her hands crept round his back and she could feel the thunder of his heartbeat against her breasts.

Finally he lifted his head and she touched her lips compulsively against his throat, feeling him tremble against her. He looked down into her eyes as she put back her head, his gaze holding her till she felt she would drown in the green of his eyes, their pupils enlarging darkly, his look holding her captive at the same moment as his arms fell from her body.

'It will be light soon,' he said roughly, and turned away. 'I can't stay here any longer. Get dressed. We're going.'

Wordlessly she did as he asked, zipping up her anorak and wrapping herself into the blanket he held out to her.

Moments later he doused the light and lifted the sledge down from the wall. They walked out of the hut as the glimmer of dawn streaked the darkness of the night sky.

CHAPTER FOUR

THE days that followed were strangely unreal. Almost mechanically Sophie went through the motions of everyday living. The children were fed, walked, bathed and dressed while she responded outwardly to their questions and their needs. But at night, lying in bed, she allowed her turmoil to surface, her thoughts returning constantly to Max and the time they had spent in the small hut in the mountains.

Over and over she wondered if she had been wise to let him go away. Perhaps even a few weeks with him would have been better than this terrible void, this reluctance to go on living at all without him. Yet why was she so shattered? Had her first brush with sexual passion thrown her off balance? Was it possible her feelings were more than sexual infatuation? The emotions he had aroused in her were so entirely new that she had no yardstick with which to measure them. She had never felt anything like it for any man. Could that account for her inability to forget him? Or could it be that she had fallen in love with him?

She could find no answers, and night after night her thoughts continued to ramble, giving her no peace and little sleep.

And the house was a shell without him. The children's father came and went. When he was with them they clamoured round him, demanding his attention, wanting him to play, to ski, to talk or just to cuddle. But his mind, too, seemed to be elsewhere. He looked drawn and was unresponsive. Vaguely Sophie wondered what could be the trouble.

It was a week after the avalanche that she finally came out of her nightmare world. Walking unexpectedly into the childrens' day nursery, she saw them huddled in a corner, whispering. At her entrance they stopped talking, their faces guilty as they crouched away from her. Slightly dazed, she touched a hand to her head. What was she doing? These two had enough unhappiness with the break-up of their family and the illness of a familiar nanny, without adding to their confusion. She had to snap out of it and give them the energy and care they needed.

'What about tea downstairs in front of the fire?' she suggested lightly, and they thawed immediately, throwing themselves at her in their enthusiasm. When consulted, Lisl entered into the spirit of the adventure and lit a fire in the living-room. Even the two dachshunds were allowed into the house. They toasted bread in the flames from the logs and nothing had ever tasted so good to the children as they munched and talked, the dogs blissfully asleep at their side.

The next morning they all woke to thick snow. The heavy flakes fell in a white cloud past the window panes and there was no question of ski school. Later they would build a snowman, but the morning would be spent inside. Sophie blessed her foresight in bringing games, and dug out her Monopoly.

They had never played before, and Erika was querulous, finding difficulty in understanding the rules. But Emil was in his element. For the first time Sophie saw him fully stretched, his mind racing ahead, calculating, considering and triumphant with every gain.

'I'll take the bank now,' he announced loftily after

the first game. 'You two can play together. I'll take you both on.'

The morning passed in a flash and they all looked up in surprise when Lisl appeared to announce lunch.

'As you're all down here,' she said hesitantly, looking at Sophie, 'I thought perhaps you might like to eat in the kitchen?'

There was a tense silence as three pairs of blue eyes swivelled to stare at Sophie. She could hear the children hold their breath as they waited for her decision. She guessed it was forbidden, but she hadn't the heart to deny them.

'What a good idea,' she said calmly, and found herself almost knocked over in the rush as the children headed for the kitchen, the dogs barking excitedly at their heels.

The two women looked at each other. Lisl shrugged and then grinned at Sophie, who smiled back.

'It is good,' Lisl said, 'you are coming back to the living.'

That evening the children were asleep as soon as their heads touched the pillows. Even Emil unbent, and gave her a quick hug as she bent to kiss him goodnight.

The afternoon had continued the good humour of the morning. The snow was still falling and continued too soft to build a snowman, but they had dressed and popped out into the garden to indulge in a fierce snowball fight, bringing colour to their cheeks before they tumbled back into the house ravenous for their evening meal.

Sophie was in her room, warm and changed into slacks when a soft knock broke through her thoughts.

It was Lisl, but without the usual supper tray.

'I . . . I thought,' she began shyly, 'I mean—if you like—I've made a schnitzel for supper and I wondered if you—I mean you're all alone . . .'

'Could I come down and eat with you?' Sophie asked.

'Yes, it would be nice. We are both alone: Peter is not in tonight.'

Downstairs the table was set for two with wine, and Sophie smiled in appreciation at the younger girl as Lisl began to dish up and they sat down.

'Where is Peter?' Sophie tried to break the slight awkwardness.

'With his girl-friend. They marry this summer and all the time they sit in each other's lap.' Lisl grinned, her face wide with appreciation at her own joke.

'What about you?' Sophie asked.

'I, too, will be married, but not till next year. My Franz is doing his—how do you say?—military service. He comes back at Christmas and we marry in the spring. It all works well because Peter and Christl will live here after they marry and he takes over from me. My Franz and I will work for his parents in the family hotel. One day he will inherit,' Lisl added proudly. 'He is the only son.'

'So will Christl mind spending her married life here with the von Hartogs instead of having her own home?'

'They will have a flat. It is being prepared. The Herr Baron permits them their furniture, so it will be a home. And all the year there is no one, only the dogs. Just at Christmas and for the skiing the family come.'

Sophie found her interest caught, and was eating with enjoyment the veal with *Rösti*, the small crisply fried potatoes, and the traditional cucumber salad that Lisl had prepared.

'So it is an easy job?' Sophie asked.

'Yes and no. It has not been a happy house since the family divorced.' She sat back and sighed. 'That was last year. The Herr Doktor, he took it hard when his wife left. She is very beautiful, the children's mother. And now there is no mistress.'

Sophie bent her head to her plate. 'But the master—the Herr Baron—he will marry and then there'll be a mistress again?'

'Oh, no, he won't marry now,' Lisl said firmly. 'Once many years ago there was ... I mean,' she flushed, 'I don't know of course, but Peter told me the Herr Baron, he loved very much. But she married someone else.'

'Oh, I see,' said Sophie inadequately, her imagination in a whirl. Resolutely she clamped down on her thoughts. 'This is lovely, Lisl, and it tastes much better down here with you.' She sighed extravagantly. 'I've eaten too much.'

Lisl smiled. 'Coffee?'

'Yes, please.'

Lisl had her back to Sophie, stacking dishes. 'You know,' she said carefully, 'we all worry about you— after the avalanche. It was so terrible. You looked so— what is the word?—broken. And the master, he also was down—very tired when he left. It was a bad thing.' She turned to smile at Sophie. 'But now it is perhaps behind you?' she asked quaintly.

'Yes, thank you, Lisl,' said Sophie evenly. 'Now it is behind me.'

Later that night, as she lay sleeplessly in the dark, her thoughts returned to Lisl's artless revelations. So Max had loved a girl who'd married another man. She wondered how long ago it was. Was that why he had not married? Had the girl been beautiful, she thought painfully, someone of his world, to grace his home and be the centre of his life, the mother of his children ...

Silently the tears came, and Sophie turned her face into the pillow.

'Why don't you have a good run, Sophie?' asked Lisl a few days later. 'You've only three days left and the sun is beautiful this morning. I'll keep an eye on the children. And you've had no free time this week. I envy you your skiing; I hear the master say how good it is.'

Sophie blushed and turned away. The two girls had come to know each other in the past week, an easy companionship developing between them. Even the children felt it and had relaxed, taking over the house and running carelessly from room to room, voices raised in happy laughter. One afternoon they had invaded the kitchen and made fudge, leaving cutlery, pans and tabletops sticky with sugar. The snowman had been finished and now stood fat and shapeless inside the front gate. Peter, doing odd jobs round the house, didn't interfere.

When he first returned from his weekend leave he had been appalled at the informality of the household. Sophie had heard his voice raised in anger as he scolded his sister, and had wondered if she should go down and interfere, to defend Lisl from his anger. But listening to their voices, trying to disentangle the Austrian dialect, she had realised that Lisl was well able to hold her own against her brother. And she had left them to it. When next she saw Lisl she had asked tentatively if she would prefer things to return to what they had been, but Lisl had snorted indignantly.

No brother of hers was going to tell her how to behave. Once the master was back or the Herr Doktor in residence everything would return to the more ordered household as he would wish. For the moment things were fine as they were. The children were happier than she could remember, and Peter could mind his own business.

'You haven't skied since the accident,' Lisl was saying. 'It is important to ski again quickly to keep your nerve.'

'Perhaps.' Sophie was non-committal. She didn't want to ski again this year, not because of the accident, but because it would bring reminders of Max, of the time they'd spent together in the mountains, of the touch of his hands and his lips and the beautiful words he had used to tell her of his feelings, all memories that would remain with her for a very long time.

She had cancelled her skiing holiday and booked a flight home as soon as her time at the von Hartog villa was finished. She had no wish to stay in Kitzbühl and run the risk of seeing Max again.

'Sophie, it's late; we must go.' The children demanded her attention and she pushed her personal problems to the back of her mind.

They were all three trudging back up the hill to the house, Sophie carrying Erika's skis as well as her own, when the little girl suddenly stopped and shouted.

'Emil, look,' she cried out in German. 'It's *Mutti! Mutti!*' she screamed, and ran.

Emil stood quite still with shock, his blue eyes enormous in his small face. Sophie touched him lightly on the arm.

'I'll bring your skis, Emil, if you want to run

ahead.' He seemed to come out of his trance. With a swift, rather desperate look at her, he dropped his skis and ran after his sister.

Sophie picked up all the skis and put them over her shoulders, wondering if Nanny Elisabeth had arrived with her mistress. The big sleigh stood in front of the house, its red upholstery luxurious against the shiny black of the horses. Peter emerged from the side of the house and climbed up into it, waving his hand in greeting before he drove off round the back of the garden to the stables.

She stacked the skis in the stand by the side door and let herself into the house. The hall was piled high with luggage, and from the living-room she could hear the excited voices of the children mingling with a woman's low tones. Upstairs she changed back into her uniform, and half an hour later, when the nursery wing was looking spick and span, she made her way downstairs to see if she could help Lisl with the unexpected influx.

The cases had disappeared from the hall and the house seemed oddly silent. As she hesitated, Peter came out from the kitchen and nodded to her.

'I was just coming up to find you. The Frau Doktor would like to see you.'

'Thank you, Peter.'

Sophie realised that she was slightly nervous of meeting the children's mother. Walking past the big mirror in the hall, she straightened up, checked her appearance and told herself firmly not to be silly. She wasn't a schoolgirl about to be scolded. She was an experienced nanny. She knocked and walked in.

The children were sitting on the sofa, side by side. Before she could look round for their mother, a man rose from a chair by the window. Tall, broad and strangely forbidding, Max von Hartog stood still and bowed formally, his eyes indifferent, his face a polite blank.

The shock went right through her body. She could feel it in every quivering nerve. She had not expected to see him again—ever. And now he was back, obviously intent on being only the master of the house, treating her with cool courtesy. Why had he come back? Why couldn't he have waited till she'd gone? she thought hopelessly, fighting the elation she felt at the sight of him. She pulled herself together, tearing her eyes from his face to study the woman sitting by the fire in an upright chair.

'Dorothea, this is Miss Carter, who has been looking after the children.'

Dorothea von Hartog was beautiful. Tall and slender with ash-blonde hair, she was elegantly dressed in a soft wool suit of lilac with a toning silk blouse, the colour emphasising the fair complexion and the wide blue eyes. Those eyes now surveyed Sophie with cool disdain.

'You're very large,' she said at last, 'however do you manage with the children?'

It was a personal comment and it was rude, but Sophie did not react to the tactless remark.

'Please take the children now,' the Frau Doktor said dismissively, and got up. 'They're late for their lunch.'

Sophie beckoned to the children, holding out a hand to each as their mother walked across to her cousin. The children hesitated, looking longingly across at their mother, but she was giving all her attention to Maximilian von Hartog.

'Max, *Liebling*, will you please . . .' She stopped and looked across the room at Sophie. 'Are you waiting for something?' she demanded coolly.

Sophie walked over to the children and shepherded them out of the room.

'Are you going to take me out to lunch now, Max, darling? This house is like a mausoleum.' Sophie closed the door on Max von Hartog's reply.

The next hour was spent coaxing the children to eat, watching their set faces during the curiously silent meal. She asked no questions and made casual remarks about everyday events, until they had managed to eat something and she had them in bed. Erika clung fiercely as Sophie bent to tuck her in, and she sat down beside the little girl, who was fighting to keep back her tears.

'Come, you're tired,' said Sophie gently. 'You'll feel better when you've had a rest.'

Erika transferred her clinging arms to the best-loved teddy and closed her eyes obediently, ready for sleep. In Emil's room Sophie closed the shutters, wondering what to do about the rigid face and tense figure lying in the narrow bed. He was a loner, this little boy, too young and vulnerable to be ignored by a father who probably meant no harm, but was lost in his own misery. How she could reach him and whether she could help in the odd days left to her was something she didn't know. She had no wish to start a relationship which would leave him bereft when she too came to leave. But how could she bear to see him like this and do nothing?

She sat down on the edge of his bed.

'I'll be next door if you want me, Emil,' she said softly.

He transferred his rigid gaze from the ceiling to her face. 'Thank you,' he replied stiffly.

'May I stay for a moment?' She changed her

tactics. At that he did give her his attention. 'I like this room,' she went on. 'It's like you, quiet and restful.'

His look became intent. 'Do you think she's beautiful?' he asked awkwardly.

'Very,' replied Sophie without hesitation.

'Yes,' he said, his mouth quivering. 'Uncle Max thinks so too.'

Sophie sat quite still. What did he mean? she wondered.

'Anyone would consider her beautiful,' she said slowly. 'You must be very proud of her.'

'No!' he said fiercely. 'I hate her!'

'Emil!' Sophie was shocked.

'Oh, not like Erika because she doesn't love us. I got over that years ago,' he said airily, his mouth tight, his eyes wet. 'I hate her for what she does to Papa.' Sophie sat quietly, wondering if it was good for the boy to talk to her like this. 'I think she's going to marry Uncle Max,' he added.

Sophie uttered a smothered cry which she turned into a cough as the child's huge eyes became suddenly intent on her face.

'Surely not,' she managed at last.

'That's why she left Papa,' he announced rigidly. 'I know.' His eyes returned to the ceiling. 'I heard Lisl and Peter talking. They didn't know I was behind the door. She and Uncle Max were engaged once, a long time ago before I was born. Then something happened—I don't know what. They didn't say. And she married Papa. And Papa adores her; he always has. He's not interested in us . . . only her. And she left because she doesn't care for any of us—only Uncle Max.'

Her own pain forgotten, Sophie reached blindly for the boy, and he let her hold him as he began to sob, brokenly and wretchedly. She sat on, murmuring soothingly, holding him gently and letting him cry. Finally he quietened and his head became heavy against her. He had fallen asleep. Thank God, she thought, as she laid him back and covered him. The small face was somehow peaceful, still wet with tears, but not so rigid, so controlled. She hoped he wouldn't regret having talked to her.

She got up and tiptoed to her own room, leaving the door ajar in case he woke. She would miss the children, she thought sadly. In the short time she had known them they had each found a special place in her heart; Erika with her emotions spilling everywhere, her need to be cuddled and her longing for approval; and Emil, so much more complicated than his sister, sensitive and vulnerable, far too mature for his years. Both were discovering early in life that loving could bring pain, and strangely she wished she could stay with them, perhaps help them through a difficult time in their lives. Erika would survive. In many ways she was like her mother. But Emil was too fragile, like his father, only too clearly aware of his mother's indifference.

But surely he had to be wrong about that? Careless of her children's feelings she might be, but she must love them. How could a mother not do so?

Restlessly she got up. The house was wrapped in silence. No voices penetrated from below, and she wondered vaguely where Lisl could be. But she didn't move. She had no appetite for lunch, and her thoughts returned again to Emil, to his artless words that had revealed so much.

Was Dorothea the woman Lisl had meant when she said Max had once been in love with a girl who had married someone else? It was quite possible. Certainly he had been ill at ease downstairs. Sophie had watched him too often in the past to be mistaken about that. And his indifference with her had been genuine. Had he been embarrassed, having to meet her again in the company of the woman he loved? She threw back her head to stem the tears she could feel, damp on her lashes. Dorothea was beautiful enough to turn any man's head, she thought painfully.

There was a soft knock on the door. Lisl stood in the doorway, and Sophie put a finger to her lips indicating the children were asleep.

'I'm so sorry,' Lisl whispered. 'Everything's disorganised and I forgot to bring your food.'

'Come in.' Sophie moved over to shut the nursery door. 'I finally managed to get Emil off to sleep,' she explained quietly.

Lisl was plainly not listening.

'I wish they'd let me know they were coming,' she said in German. 'Nothing was ready—food, beds— nothing,' she repeated. 'It's not like the master to be inconsiderate.' She sighed. 'Anyway, I came to tell you there's some soup downstairs if you wish.' Anxiously she looked up into Sophie's face, her mind clearly elsewhere.

'Don't worry about me, Lisl. I'm not hungry. If I want something later I'll come down and get it.'

The relief relaxed Lisl's worried face and she turned to go. Outside in the corridor Peter was hovering uncertainly.

'What is it?' his sister demanded rather sharply.

'I've been sent to tell Miss Sophie to come down— er—at once,' he added awkwardly. 'The mistress wants to see her.'

'Thank you, Peter, I'll be right down.'

Sophie closed the door behind them and checked

her appearance. A quick wash, a spray of cologne and she was ready.

'*Herein*,' the voice called as she knocked, and Sophie was relieved to see that the Frau Doktor was alone.

'I wish to talk to you,' she began formally. 'Please come in.'

Sophie walked into the middle of the room, her hands under her apron in the pockets of her dress, her face calm, her eyes firmly on the face of her employer's ex-wife. She was not asked to sit down.

'I'm not happy about the children and I want to know what has been going on here,' the other woman began. 'They are noisy and rude. They talk of strange games with money and making toast in here before the fire. It is all most worrying and I am seriously displeased.'

Sophie did not comment.

'You say nothing?' The Frau Doktor looked up in surprise. 'Have you no wish to apologise?'

'I'm an experienced nanny, *gnädige Frau*, and I don't believe I have anything for which to apologise.'

'Now you're being impertinent!'

'I had no such intention.'

'I think you have been permitted too much freedom in this house,' Dorothea von Hartog continued. 'You forget you are here to work, not to be indulged by the Herr Baron.'

Sophie looked up in surprise.

'I understand you have taken advantage of his kindness, begging him to take you on his outings with the children. And he is too much of a gentleman to object—whatever his feelings. He is always considerate of his servants, so it is left to me to tell you of those feelings.'

Sophie looked away from those large cold eyes as she felt the colour flush her face. Dorothea's voice was soft and low as though she was discussing the weather, and Sophie determined to keep her cool. She would not lose her temper with this arrogant woman, or trade insults with her. Since she could hardly inform the Frau Doktor that she was lying, it was best to say nothing.

'I think it is better if you go,' the older woman said after a moment, her voice unexpectedly vehement. Sophie looked back at her in surprise.

'I shall be leaving when my employment ends on Saturday,' she pointed out politely.

'I mean now. Right away. Today. I wish you to go.'

'You will recall it was the Herr Doktor who employed me,' Sophie said quietly. 'He would be the one to terminate my employment.'

'It seems you do not know your place, and this I regret. But it makes it even more necessary for you to leave. I will not permit you to ruin my children.' The Austrian woman smoothed the cuffs of her suit with the fingers of one hand, looking intently down at her immaculate red fingernails. 'Since I am the children's mother, I assure you I have the right and the power to make you leave. Naturally you will be paid everything owing to you.'

'Very well,' Sophie said after a moment. 'Perhaps you could explain to the children . . .'

The door opened behind Sophie.

'There you are, Max darling,' Dorothea von Hartog broke in. 'Please help me,' she pleaded, pursing her mouth in childish misery. 'I'm having trouble with this—person. She is being impertinent.'

Sophie stood quite still, all too achingly aware of the man standing suddenly so close behind her. She stiffened as she heard his voice, affectionate, indulgent and gentle.

'My dear, I'm sure Miss Carter has no wish to be rude.' He walked past Sophie and his sleeve brushed her arm. She flinched sharply away from the contact, and Frau von Hartog saw the movement. Her eyes narrowed and her mouth thinned, and Sophie wanted only to get away from that hard-eyed stare and the presence of the man now standing beside the beautiful woman. Side by side they looked ideally matched. His towering, formidable good looks and her porcelain beauty.

'Excuse me,' Sophie murmured. 'I have to pack.' She turned and walked away from them both, a sudden bitterness in her mouth. Without warning came pain, and with it her first taste of jealousy—and envy. It clutched at her heart and blocked her throat.

'Just a moment.' It was Max.

She stopped but didn't turn.

'Did you say pack?' he demanded.

'Yes, darling. I've asked her to leave.' Sophie turned to see Dorothea put her hand affectionately on his arm, her face turned up to him. 'I don't want her near the children. Some of the things that have been going on ... I'll tell you later.'

'I see,' he said flatly. 'Is Nanny Elisabeth arriving today, then, to take charge?'

'Well, no, she's not quite well yet, but Lisl can take care of the children till she arrives.'

He turned to look down at her. 'I'm afraid that won't be possible, my dear,' he said smoothly. 'Lisl will have her hands full with this party tomorrow night.'

'But we can get extra help, can't we?' she coaxed him, smiling provocatively into his eyes.

'That I have done,' he explained, 'but Lisl will be supervising all the arrangements and there's a lot to do. We haven't given them a great deal of notice, you'll recall.'

His look down into her face was not that of a lover, and Sophie wondered that the woman didn't quail at the hard, implacable face.

'Very well,' said Dorothea at last, 'whatever you think best. Don't be angry with me, Max,' she pleaded tearfully. 'You know how miserable it makes me.'

Sophie turned her head away as she heard Max's voice.

'I don't wish to upset you, my dear,' he said, 'but we have to face facts. I believe Miss Carter is leaving us in any case at the weekend. By then Lisl will have the time to take over in case Nanny isn't with us yet.'

Sophie broke into this explanation.

'So what do you wish me to do?' she asked woodenly.

'I would be grateful if you stayed for the next days as planned,' he said formally.

'Grateful?' The other woman was incredulous. 'You seem to forget you're speaking to a servant!'

'Thank you, Miss Carter.'

Sophie heard the anger in his voice, but knew it wasn't directed at her. As she closed the door behind her the voices continued in the room she'd left. She breathed in deeply before making her way upstairs, walking slowly to let her agitation subside.

She wasn't sure if she was pleased at Max's intervention. Staying in this house was becoming more difficult each day since he had returned, and it might have been better to leave right away, not to see him again.

Why had he come back? she wondered again. Was it to escort the beautiful woman downstairs? Did they have an understanding now that she was no longer his cousin's wife? And did he plan to marry her? What then of the feelings he had professed for her up in the mountains the day of the avalanche? Had that been merely a passing desire, or a brief infatuation which died when she refused him?

Restlessly she walked up and down in her room. Would her feelings also die a natural death once she returned to the familiarity of London? Or would her emotions remain to torment her with what might have been? She didn't know the answer, and hadn't the will to analyse her feelings as she did so often. There would be time enough when she was back home to measure her pain and loss.

Standing by the window, she looked out at the snow. The sun was sinking fast, as it did in the winter months, throwing deep shadows across the town below, and bringing the cold of winter into the narrow streets. Distantly she could hear bells tinkling as the cows came down from milking to head back to their warm, straw-filled stables.

For her, Kitzbühl would never be the same. She had loved it in the past and had enjoyed coming back each winter. But she would not return. Her next skiing holiday would be in the Italian Alps, far away from the Hahnenkamm with its many painful memories.

CHAPTER FIVE

THE children were restless and irritable. Preparations for the party had been in progress all day and the excitement affected everyone. Even the dogs were whining, sensitive to the highly charged atmosphere.

'Stand still, Erika,' protested Sophie. 'How can I tie this if you keep twisting?'

They were to go down early in the evening to spend an hour at the party, a treat that had been wrung reluctantly from their mother. Emil was nervous and flushed with excitement. Since their talk the previous day, he had been more relaxed, although the return of his father had sent him for a while into a frenzy of anxiety. The fear of his father's hurt seemed to touch him as though it was his own.

During the afternoon Sophie had been relieved to have a couple of hours free and decided to go out. Changing into boots and her suede sheepskin coat, she had let herself out of the house, eager to enjoy an hour away from the villa among the crowds that thronged the cafés and shops. She had walked briskly, watching the lights of the ski lift as the chairs moved slowly, taking up the last of the skiers, the ones who were prepared to risk a descent in the half dark.

In town the roads were slippery, the snow melting under the imprint of chain-protected tyres and the boots of tourists trudging wearily back to their hotels after a day's skiing. She chose a large, fashionable café, its tables outside now empty, and sat inside near the window to watch the town gradually moving into evening, lights springing up as hotels prepared for the festivities ahead.

Sipping the steaming coffee with its topping of cream, she began to relax. The café was crowded, waitresses in black, their small white aprons flapping, huge trays held high as they moved expertly among the tables and the noise of clamouring customers. Sophie opened the London paper she had bought and scanned the news.

'*Ist dieser Platz frei?*'

She looked up to see a young man waiting for her consent to sit at the table.

She nodded. '*Ja, bitte.*'

'You're English,' he said as he sat down.

'That's right.'

'My luck must be in,' he grinned. 'I've been in this Godforsaken place for a week with not a soul to talk to.'

'That must be a record,' she replied. 'People to talk to here are two a penny. One morning in the ski school and you'd have met a dozen.'

'Oh, sure,' he looked sheepish, 'but I'm—I don't go to ski school. I'm a competition skier. I go on my own.'

'I'm impressed,' she responded lightly.

'Listen, can I buy you a—whatever you're having, and talk to you for a minute?'

Sophie hesitated. She was really out to enjoy some privacy, but he was regarding her with such melting charm from twinkling blue eyes that she found herself laughing and saying yes.

'I'm in terrible trouble,' he began without preamble.

'You look pretty cheerful about it,' she commented.

'Yeah, well, I don't really know much about women ...'

'Woman trouble?'

'Mm ...' He paused, his face serious, his hands clasped on the table. 'My girl back home—I'm from Toronto—we had a Godawful row.' He sighed. 'After this season I want to go professional, and that means a nomadic life.' He smiled faintly. 'We plan to marry in the spring, but all she can think about is a house and furniture—and babies.'

'That's pretty normal.'

'I know that. And I want it too, but not yet. She's only nineteen. Why can't she wait?'

'Well, why can't she? Have you asked her?'

'Family,' he said cryptically. 'She won't leave her folks. Wants a house in the same road, for God's sake!' He sighed. 'I'm pretty easy going, but she has to grow up.'

'So what happened?' asked Sophie gently. 'Did you just walk out on her?'

He nodded, a slight flush rising under his tan.

'I ... I gave her an ultimatum,' he admitted sheepishly.

'Oh.' Sophie considered his words. 'I think I'd have been livid,' she said softly. 'In fact I think I'd have flung your ring back.'

'You would?' He stared in astonishment. 'That's exactly what she did!'

Sophie smiled faintly. 'So you took her in your arms, told her how much you love her and that anything she wanted was all right with you.'

There was a moment's silence and then he smiled, a slightly rueful grin. 'That's what I should have done?'

'You didn't?'

'Hell, no.' His grin disappeared. 'She can't have whatever she wants. I'm not a fairy godfather; I'll be her husband.'

'And do you think that's something she can understand—before you're married?' she asked quietly.

'Now why didn't I think of that?' he asked softly, and leaned towards her across the table. He picked up her hand and bent to kiss her fingers lightly. 'Thank you,' he murmured.

Over his head Sophie looked straight into the face of Maximilian von Hartog. He was at the counter waiting to be served, and she stared at him in amazement. His expression was icy, his lips drawn into a thin line of anger, his face taut with contempt. The look lasted only a moment before the boy at her table raised his head and Max turned away. But Sophie felt as though she'd been slapped. The blood drained from her face and the room began to swim round her.

'Are you all right?' her companion asked anxiously. 'You look a bit ... it isn't anything I said, is it?'

'No,' she managed, and shook her head. 'But I don't feel too good. I think I'd better get back.'

'I'll see you home.'

An hour later Sophie was on her way down to collect the children. She was crossing the hall when Max came out of his study.

'I wish to see you for a moment,' he said tightly.

'I have to fetch the children,' she answered him.

'Now,' he said grimly, and she walked past him into the room. She had not seen the study; it was out of bounds to the children. She was briefly conscious of warm brown panelling, thick tweed curtains and a wide modern desk before Max closed the door and remained with his back to it.

'What is it?' she asked nervously.

'Who was that young man?' he asked tautly.

Sophie resisted the temptation to say what young man and remained silent.

'Well?' he demanded.

'Your question is personal and I have no intention of answering it.' She looked up into his face, her own calm, her eyes clear, showing no sign of the turmoil she felt in his presence. He moved past her to the window.

'While you're in this house I—we—have some responsibility for your welfare. If anything happened to you we'd be blamed.' When she didn't speak, he turned round. 'Well?' he asked again.

'Are you asking me if I agree?'

'Do you?'

'No,' she said baldly. 'My personal life is not your concern.'

'Do you know no one has ever talked to me like this?' he demanded angrily.

'I could say the same. I'm not used to having my life questioned by my employers.'

'Do you have any idea how angry you make me?'

It was such a childish remark that her face softened. All she wanted was to caress the tension from his face, to coax him out of his angry mood. She couldn't seem to be angry with him for long, and wished fleetingly that she had more strength to control her feelings.

Max was looking at her, and she saw the anger leave his eyes. His face relaxed and she sensed danger. Swiftly she veiled her eyes. He must not know how deeply and immediately he could tap her emotions, how much she longed for his tenderness and yearned to be close to him.

'Sophie . . .' he began, but she cut him short.

'I have to go,' she said curtly, turning away from him.

'No.'

In two strides he was at her side. She flinched, but didn't move away, fearing to rouse him further. Then he turned her into his arms and she felt the full length of his body against her.

'Dear God, Sophie, what am I going to do with you?' He bent his head to her lips, but she moved, evading the searching mouth. 'What's this? Do I repel you now?' he demanded savagely. 'Is the blond youth more to your liking?' He held her away from him. 'Are you fickle? Is that why you won't commit yourself to me?'

She turned her face up to his, unable to keep up the cool pretence. 'Oh, Max,' she whispered, and was snatched back into his arms, all restraint gone as he fastened his lips to hers, bruising and demanding. Savagely he invaded her mouth, refusing her breath as his arms tightened round her body and she felt the hard length of his legs against hers, intimate, intoxicating.

The blood thundered in her ears and she threw back her head under the pressure of his mouth, her hands creeping up to his shoulders and into his hair, feeling the shape of him under her fingers. Desire for him swept her into a sudden vortex of emotion as his hand moved down her back.

'Max!'

The voice cracked into the silence and Sophie came back to earth with shattering suddenness. He took his arms away and pushed past her. Running a hand through his hair, he whipped out of the door, closing it firmly behind him, giving her a chance to recover as he faced Dorothea in the hall.

'There you are! The nanny's disappeared again,' she complained. 'She was supposed to collect the children and she's late. I told you we should have let her go.'

'Do you want me to find her for you?' he asked, his voice low and controlled.

'It doesn't matter. I'll send Lisl.'

By this time Sophie had her hair tucked back under her cap and her clothes tidy. Max opened the door and nodded wordlessly. She slipped past him into the empty hall.

'There, that's it,' Sophie said to Erika. 'Now your hair and you're ready.'

'Please hurry,' begged the little girl.

'Come on, Erika,' her brother moaned. 'We'll be late!'

With deft fingers Sophie fixed the plaits, twining the blue ribbon through the blonde thickness.

'That's it. All done,' she said finally as Erika tugged to get away. 'And remember, young ladies do not rush down the stairs. They walk slowly so that everyone will look at them.'

'Truly, Sophie?' The little girl looked up at Sophie.

'Certainly. Your mother is beautiful and admired. You don't see her rushing about, do you?'

'No . . .' The child considered thoughtfully.

'If you don't come, Erika, I'll go without you,' her brother threatened, and the next moment both children were scampering down the stairs.

In her sitting-room, Sophie drew back the curtains and reached out to push aside the shutters. There was a hush over the sleeping landscape, and lights were twinkling back at her from the darkness. She should be packing, she thought vaguely, but she didn't move. She was tired; the day had been full.

Dorothea von Hartog she had seen only once during the afternoon. They had passed each other on the stairs, and the older woman had stopped her with an imperious movement of the hand.

'We—my husband and I—wish you to join the party this evening,' she said stiffly, as though the words had been forced from her.

'Thank you, but I have packing to do and would ask you to excuse me.'

The relief in the other woman's face had been instant, and Sophie wondered who had demanded she issue the invitation.

Faintly she could hear the pianist playing on the grand in the music room, but felt no wish to join the party. Leaning back in her chair, she closed her eyes.

'Sophie?'

It was Lisl at the door, peering in, wondering if she was asleep in the unlit room.

'You're wanted. The children are to come upstairs.'

Voices floated out through the open double doors of the sitting-room, and Sophie could see Dorothea bending down to the children, who were arguing. Erika, she could see, was in tears.

'For goodness' sake, where have you been?' Dorothea snapped. 'Take them upstairs now. It's late.'

'Certainly,' said Sophie quietly. 'Come on, you two. I've a treat upstairs.' She shepherded them to the door.

'What is it, Sophie? Please tell us!' Erika's voice was strident with nervous excitement.

'There isn't anything,' said Emil scornfully. 'It's just a trick to get us upstairs.'

'Well, I certainly hope it isn't a trick. I'd hate it to disappear when I've taken so much trouble to get it ready,' Sophie replied gently, aware of the controlled tension in the boy's face. 'What would you say to a midnight feast?' They both stood still, their heads swivelling to stare up at her.

'Truly?' breathed Erika.

'Our own party,' she said. 'Unless we ask the dogs.'

'Yes!' they chorused, and rushed up the stairs ahead of her. In the nursery they stopped. There was nothing. Sophie turned them to face her room.

'Close your eyes and keep them closed.'

They shut their eyes tight and she put a match to the candles. 'Now,' she said. They opened their eyes, staring in wide-eyed amazement, and suddenly Sophie was fiercely glad she had taken the trouble.

A small cake stood in the centre of the table, a swirl of cream forming their names: Emil and Erika. Set amidst more candles were sandwiches, fingers of toast, little fondant creams—everything exactly as the buffet downstairs.

'Oh, Sophie, our own party!' Erika was ecstatic.

Sophie pressed the button on her small cassette recorder and low piano music tinkled softly. And still the children stood motionless, candlelight gleaming on their excited faces.

'Well,' asked Sophie at last. 'Anyone hungry?'

Nearly two hours later she had them in bed, overfed, exhausted and reasonably happy. She was clearing away in the kitchen when she heard the suppressed sniffle. In Erika's room she sat down on the bed and took the unhappy bundle into her arms.

'What's all this?' she asked softly. 'We have a party and it makes you cry?'

'You're going home tomorrow, aren't you?' came the muffled reply.

'Is that what this is all about?' she asked in surprise. 'I may be going, but you've your own nanny coming back, and your mummy here. That's more than most little girls have.'

'Mummy doesn't like me.' The tortured whisper seemed to be wrung from her.

'Now you know that's not true,' said Sophie calmly, hiding her consternation. Both children seemed so certain of this. Erika lifted a tear-stained face.

'You won't tell her I said so, will you?' she pleaded.

'I never tell secrets,' Sophie answered gravely.

'She thinks I don't know,' Erika went on, 'but I do. Emil knows too. She likes him a little, but she doesn't like me at all. I'm not good and she hates me to kiss her.'

Sophie took the child in her arms to soothe and quieten her, wondering what she could tell the sensitive little girl.

'Your mummy has a lot to think about, you know,' she said gently.

'Has she?'

'All mothers are busy people and they don't always have time to play and cuddle. But your mummy's very proud of you, and she wants you to grow up to be clever and well behaved.'

A smothered sniffle reached Sophie, and she smoothed the disordered hair back from the small face. 'You're going to be very beautiful, you know, and that's something you have from your mother. Just think how much you'll enjoy being grown up and admired. I bet when you're sixteen you'll have all the boys wanting to take you out.'

'I hate boys. They're all like Emil,' Erika informed her crossly.

'If you're going to look like that no one will admire you, so it'll be just as well if you don't like them.' Sophie leaned over and picked up a hand mirror. 'Here,' she said, 'look at your face.' Erika shook her head. 'It looks like this,' Sophie said, and pulled a hideous grimace.

'Oh, Sophie, you look awful!'

'So, just imagine if I had that expression all the time. You'd run away, wouldn't you?'

'I don't know,' the little girl said thoughtfully. 'I might get used to it—if you were kind.'

Sophie leaned forward and kissed her lightly. 'And now it's time for sleep. Come on, cuddle down with teddy. I'll stay for a minute.'

'Till I'm asleep?' Erika pleaded.

'A little while,' repeated Sophie firmly.

The child's hand in hers, she sat in the dark, the night light flickering sending shadows on to the ceiling, the shape of toys and furniture strangely distorted.

Children.

Her throat contracted. Heartache there was in plenty when one was little. She sighed, the feeling of tiredness returning. A slight movement caught her eye and she looked at the open door.

Max.

He stood in the shadows of the corridor, the night light reaching only the black of his evening dress and the gleam of white linen. How long had he been standing there? Had he heard the little girl?

For a long moment they stared at each other, and Sophie wished he'd go away. She couldn't face another emotional scene. This time tomorrow she would be in Munich, spending the night in some impersonal hotel, ready for the morning flight to London. And she wanted no more memories to take with her.

He beckoned to her and she got up. Smoothing the blanket across the sleeping child, she tiptoed to the door, closing it quietly behind her. Her arm was gripped tightly and he pushed her into her sitting-room, turning on the light and closing the door to the nursery. He seemed enormous in the small room, towering over her, almost menacing.

'Why aren't you downstairs?' he demanded grimly.

'I—I explained to the Frau Doktor that I . . .'

'Yes, she told me,' he interrupted. 'But I want you downstairs.'

'I'm sorry, I don't wish to come,' she said stiffly.

'I'm not interested in your wishes. I want it.'

'Please, Max, don't be difficult. You know your— the Frau Doktor doesn't want me there.'

'She is a guest in my house and has no say in the matter.' He was angry and she saw the familiar flare of his nostrils as he strove to control it.

'But why, Max? I leave tomorrow, and I really do have things to do.'

'I don't intend to stand here arguing with you. I'm not answerable to you—yet,' he stressed, and watched the colour come into her face. His eyes softened and glimmered with humour. 'I expect you downstairs in fifteen minutes—and not in that uniform. I assume you have a dress. You do occasionally wear ordinary clothes?'

She lifted her head, an angry retort on her lips, but he forestalled her. 'I'm tired, Sophie, and can't wait for this evening to end. If you're not downstairs in fifteen minutes, I'll come back here and dress you myself.'

Their eyes locked, both angry, their faces set and obstinate. Suddenly he smiled.

'I always wanted a woman with spirit. But now I've met you I'm not sure I still do,' he said ruefully.

'Oh, go away,' she said crossly.

'Fourteen and a half minutes,' Max said quietly before he closed the door behind him.

A needle-sharp shower revived her, keeping tiredness at bay, and she felt refreshed as she surveyed her meagre wardrobe. She hadn't brought much, and there were only two dresses that were vaguely suitable. She chose the green. In heavy velvet, the low neckline flattered her skin, the skirt flowing in deep folds to the tips of high-heeled evening sandals, dyed to match the dress. She curled her hair into a thick chignon against her neck and clipped on her antique earrings, a find from London's Portobello Road market, the deep red-gold gleaming against the black of her hair.

Downstairs the doors were open, people thronging from one room to another, some dancing where the floor had been cleared, others sitting with coffee cups and wine glasses. Sophie felt awkward coming into a gathering as the party appeared to be breaking up, and she wished she had ignored Max's orders and stayed upstairs. She made her way to the drinks table, more to hold a glass than because she wanted anything to drink. Behind her the music stopped.

'My dance, I think.'

Max removed the glass from her nervous fingers and guided her on to the dance floor. The pianist struck up another tune and she held herself stiffly in his arms. His look travelled across her face to the earrings. She could feel the heat rise in her body as his eyes travelled down and lingered on the V of her dress where her breasts rose and fell. Finally his glance returned to her face, noting the flush. Then he smiled.

'I like it,' he whispered, and pulled her close, moving with her to the music, his legs guiding her body and reducing her own to quivering jelly as she held on to him. With one of his arms round her back and the other holding her hand against his chest, they danced, and Sophie gave herself up to the delight of his lovemaking.

Because that was what he was doing, making love to her in public on the dance floor. She lowered her head against his shoulder and they moved as one, Max's cheek bent to her hair, his mouth at her ear.

'Isn't it lovely?' he whispered, and she trembled as his breath touched her skin, oblivious now of everything round her, aware only of his body in rhythm with hers, his heart beating under her hand and his fingers on her spine making her head spin.

Finally the music stopped. He kept his hand on her back and steered her towards the door. But she moved away as someone stopped him, determined not to be seen leaving the room with him. Across the dance floor Dorothea was staring at her. As she stood there, superbly gowned in black silk, her hair curling riotously round her face, her eyes were furious. As Sophie turned away from the malevolent stare, she wondered if Max realised how much he had angered his beautiful cousin by insisting on her own presence downstairs tonight.

She wandered out into the hall, wondering how soon she could disappear upstairs. Here was bustle and movement as guests began to leave, the front door opening briefly to admit an icy wind before it closed on another departing figure.

Through the double doors she could see Dorothea with Max. They appeared to be arguing. For a moment Sophie thought Max looked straight at her, but his face registered no recognition, and the next minute he had swung Dorothea across the dance floor and into the now deserted dining-room.

They stopped before a huge mirror, and Max had his back to her, his face reflected faintly in the glass. This would be her chance to slip away, Sophie thought, and she turned towards the stairs.

Just then Max bent his head and kissed Dorothea passionately on the mouth.

Sophie froze, her body rigid with shock as the pain rushed to her heart. As if in a nightmare she watched the two figures entwined for endless moments. Finally the dark head lifted and their eyes met.

Like a picture in slow motion, his face came into focus in the mirror. There was no sign of pleasure in his eyes, only a dark, grim determination. Then the intent stare changed as he smiled, a cruel, bitter smile, twisting his face into a grimace of triumph, as though he had achieved something he'd intended.

Was it for this he wanted her downstairs? Had he planned it all along, to show her where his real feelings lay? Or was he punishing her for her refusal of him? For a moment longer shock kept Sophie motionless.

Then she moved. Swiftly she headed for the front

door. Dragging it open, she ran out, heedless of the freezing cold or the snow that instantly penetrated her flimsy shoes.

On through the gate she went, running recklessly and then stumbling as the weight of the snow slowed her down. Tears streaming down her face, she struggled on till finally she sank down, oblivious of the cold as she fainted.

CHAPTER SIX

SHE was being carried. Strong arms were holding her against a warm body. They were climbing the back stairs, so it had to be Peter who had found her. The arms released her into a deep chair in front of a blazing fire and she began to shiver in the sudden heat. Her shoes were removed and her dress unzipped and pulled awkwardly over her head. Her arms were pushed into a woollen dressing gown and her feet tucked into a blanket. The pins were removed from her hair and her head covered with a towel. As someone began to rub her hair, her mind finally focused.

'Where am I?' Sophie asked numbly.

'In my bedroom,' said Max tonelessly.

For a moment her senses were too dulled to take it in. Then she screamed. 'No ... I ...'

His mouth covered hers, silencing her protest, and she stared at him, bemused, feeling nothing at the touch of his lips. He lifted his head and put his hand over her mouth.

'Please don't scream. You'll wake the children.'

Wide-eyed and still in shock, she nodded. Max took his hand away and moved out of her range of vision, while she sat numb, unable to think, unwilling to feel, her hands gripping the blanket that covered her legs. He pushed a glass into her hands and she drank automatically. The hot sweet tea was laced with alcohol and steadied her, but her mind remained blank and frozen even as her shivering began to subside.

'Now.' He drew up a chair, his eyes intent on her face.

She turned away. 'I want to go to my room,' she mumbled.

'And so you will—shortly.' He spoke as to a child, kind, firm and impersonal as he took the glass from her hands. 'But first we have to talk.'

'No.' The distaste washed across her face.

He didn't touch her, but neither did he move away, and she was aware of his presence, too close for comfort.

'Please,' she made to get up, 'I can't stay here.'

'This is my room and we will not be disturbed. The guests have gone and it will be assumed we are asleep in our respective beds.'

Sophie's nerves quivered at his words. Her numbed senses were returning to life and she was afraid—of what she might say and what he could do to her. He reached for her hands, but she shrank back from his touch.

'Don't touch me, please,' she whispered.

'All right, I won't touch you.' His voice was careful, controlled. 'But I want you to listen to me— hear me out.'

'No.' She looked away from him into the fire, silent, sullen.

'I had to know, Sophie,' he said, his voice suddenly urgent. 'I realise it was cruel, but I had to know,' he repeated. 'Tomorrow you would have gone and God knows when we would have met again, how long before I could have followed you.'

She looked at him, a frown between her brows, unable to follow what he was saying.

'Yes, I kissed Dorothea,' he went on grimly, 'but before I did so, I saw you in the mirror, watching us.'

'But why?' she asked helplessly. 'It was stupid—cruel.'

'I hoped to see jealousy in your face, the same jealousy I'd felt when I saw you with that handsome boy. And I had to know if you wanted me as desperately as I want you.'

'And you were successful, weren't you?' she said bitterly.

'What I didn't expect was your anguish.' His voice was low and vehement. 'I'll never forget how you looked. The surprise in your face, the shock—and the pain. I didn't realise how much—how I could hurt you,' he finished slowly. He looked across at her, the firelight creating shadows in his cheeks, his eyes shimmering with some emotion she couldn't name. 'Will you forgive me?' he whispered.

Sophie felt the tension lock in her throat; all the desperate emotions she'd tried so hard to repress were creating havoc inside her, and suddenly she lost control. Reaching her hands to cover her face, she began to cry, the silent tears trickling through her fingers as she fought to bite back the sobs that threatened.

'Oh, my dear, don't!' Max was at her side, cradling her in his arms, pulling her down on to the floor before the fire and holding her protectively. 'Perhaps I don't understand it all myself,' he said softly. 'I want you too much. It's almost as though I can't let you out of my sight in case you disappear, as though I might wake to find you gone.'

She turned to him, burying her face against him as the sobs finally escaped her control. He pulled out a handkerchief and mopped her eyes, talking to her softly till her sobs died down and the shock receded from her face. And then they sat together, huddled close, gazing into the fire.

'You won't leave me now, will you?' he asked at last, more a statement than a question.

Slowly she drew away from him and got up, the dressing gown trailing, the blanket crumpled in front of the fire as she wrapped herself into a semblance of order, pushing the hair back from her face. She stood by the window and looked out into the darkness, knowing what her answer would be. She couldn't leave him; she loved him too much. At last she acknowledged it openly. Passion was there, but infatuation it was not. Idly she wondered how long she had loved him. Had it started when he saved her that day in the mountains? Dimly she sensed she would love him always, that there could be no one else for her after Max.

So she would stay with him. Nothing could be worse than being without him. She had no experience of what an affair would do to her, but every day with him would be precious, and when he finally left her she would survive somehow and it would have to be better than having nothing of him ever.

She turned to see that he, too, had got up. He was standing with his hands in his trouser pockets, his jacket discarded with his tie, the first time she had seen him incompletely dressed. His eyes were on the fire and he didn't look happy, his face oddly grim, his jaw clenched.

'Was I wrong?' he asked quietly, and looked up. 'Do you want me? Or have I lost you?'

Sophie shook her head.

'You will stay with me—be mine?'

The question hovered in the room between them.

'I'll stay,' Sophie said quietly.

'Oh, my darling girl,' he said huskily, and moved across to take her in his arms. She leaned against him, her body suddenly weary as he held her gently. She rested her head against his shoulder, just content to be near him, to feel the hard warmth of his body against her.

Meanwhile he was talking—eagerly, his lips against her hair.

'A church ceremony, of course, but only the immediate family. Perhaps not even that. Shall we go off and be married alone? Would you like that?' He looked down at her, his face transformed, his eyes sparkling.

A further nightmare seemed to be closing in on her.

'What do you mean?' she breathed, her voice hoarse.

'We must be married—at once. We'll go to England for me to meet your family, be married and disappear. . .for a long honeymoon. Oh, God, I can't wait!'

She dropped her eyes and disentangled herself from his hold.

'I . . . I didn't realise you meant marriage,' she said unsteadily.

The silence was ominous as Max stilled. Standing close to him, she could feel his body as if braced in shock at her words.

'I don't understand,' he said tautly.

'I had no idea you meant marriage,' she said huskily.

'What did you imagine I wanted?' he asked tightly. 'An affair?' His voice was incredulous.

Sophie nodded unhappily.

'You must know I don't think of you as my

mistress.' His voice sounded almost dazed. 'I want you with me always.'

'You never told me,' she whispered.

'Is that why you refused me before—in the mountains?'

'I never thought . . .'

'You must have known,' Max accused her. 'Your experience must have told you. I could have taken you lightly at any time. We both wanted it. But I didn't because I want you as my wife, the mother of my children . . .'

'No!' She shouted for him to stop. 'No,' she repeated more quietly.

'So you thought I wanted a few weeks—months—in bed with you and then we'd go our different ways. Is that it?' he asked, a steely edge to his voice.

She turned at the severity of his tone. He was standing quite straight, his hands clenched by his side, the firelight between them.

'I don't know how you could have got that impression. Your knowledge of men must have told you I wanted more—much more than a temporary liaison.'

'My experience of men is perhaps—more limited than you imagine,' she said, her voice low.

'You're twenty-six. You can't be an innocent.'

She didn't know how to answer him. 'That doesn't matter now,' she said evasively.

'On the contrary. It matters very much.' In one swift stride Max was at her side, his hands on either side of her head, holding her face up as he scrutinised her features.

'Look at me,' he commanded as she closed her eyes. 'Sophie!' he threatened.

She opened her eyes and looked up at him, her face

rigid with tension as she tried to meet his gaze.

'It's not possible,' he muttered.

'I don't think you can blame me,' she whispered evasively. 'You never mentioned—love or marriage.'

'So now you know how I feel, have your feelings suddenly died because I want you for my wife?'

'No, my feelings are the same, but I ... I can't marry you.'

He took his hands away.

'What do you imagine we're going to do together?' He was angry now. His voice had lost its quiet deliberation and she could feel his struggle to control his anger.

'Do I rent a flat where I have visiting rights? Do you live openly with me as my mistress?'

'I don't know,' she whispered, and turned away. 'I'd have to leave the ... arrangements to you.'

'Do you fancy me, is that it?' he demanded hotly. 'You want a few weeks with me—most of them spent in bed—and then you go off to the next one? Is that what you have in mind?'

She didn't flinch at his anger or wince as he grabbed her arms, the pressure of his fingers biting cruelly into her flesh. She stood quite still in his hold making no attempt to answer him.

'You're right,' he said at last. 'We've both suffered from misunderstandings. My own feelings have been so overwhelming, I didn't stop to consider—other things.'

He released her, almost pushing her away from him, and she lost her balance and fell on to the bed behind her. He came after her, towering over her as she lay on her back, and she felt a quiver of fear at the sudden fury in his face.

'Do you know what I might do to you?' he

muttered savagely. 'Do you? You hurl your insults into my face and outstare me. Do you realise how weak you are, how much at my mercy?'

'Yes,' she said, suddenly calm and finding her voice. 'I think we should finish with this. It must be late.' She sat up. 'It would be better left till the morning.'

'We'll deal with this here and now—tonight,' Max said grimly, 'whichever way it ends.' He sat down on the bed, his hands clenched between his knees. 'Why won't you marry me?'

'I can't.'

'Why not?' he rapped out.

His tone was hard and cold and she bit her lip to hold back the tears.

'Are you married already?'

'No.'

'Is there another man you want to marry?'

Sophie shook her head. He was staring at her and her eyes dropped.

'So you don't love me as I love you,' he said flatly.

'Do you love me?' she whispered, looking up into his face.

'Yes,' he said roughly. 'I've known you only weeks, spent only hours in your company, but I knew that first evening when I walked into your room and saw you lying on the floor in those white pyjamas.' He sighed. 'And now tell me I'm insane.' He lifted a hand and ran it impatiently through his hair. 'For me the rest of my life is hardly enough time to spend with you,' he added quietly.

He loved her. She couldn't believe it. Yet he had told her—seriously, almost solemnly. Dear God, did he realise he was offering her what she most wanted on this earth, the sum total of her happiness? Warmth

spread through her body till she glowed with it and
her heartbeats quickened. Suddenly happiness was
within her grasp. She had only to reach out and take
it. She leaned forward eagerly, words trembling on
her lips ...

No. Sharply she pulled back. What was she
thinking of? It could never be, and she must not allow
herself to be tempted. Marriage with Max was not for
her. She could love him—for a while—have an affair
with him. But not marriage.

She clenched her hands to stop them reaching out
to him, and dredged up her memories of the day she
had returned to the convent where she had been born
and spent the first months of her life. She had gone to
seek her origins, to find out what she could about her
real parents. And she had been faced with the truth
about herself. At eighteen that had been hard to
accept, but now it was harder still. Now she was face
to face with the man she loved, who loved her in
return and wanted to marry her, it suddenly seemed
as though fate conspired against her, damning her
every dream, denying her all happiness.

Maximilian von Hartog could not marry a nameless girl, born of unknown, unmarried parents. Had
he been English, she might have argued that it was
not important in this day and age. But Austria was
different. And Max had an old name to honour, a title
and an inheritance to pass on to a son. And she could
never give him children. That, too, she had been told
by the nuns. So she had to refuse him, to turn away
from the happiness he offered.

'I think it best if I leave tomorrow and we agree to
part,' she said with difficulty.

'No.' He got up and began to pace the room, short
urgent strides. 'Do you want to get to know me? Live

with me first?' He stopped and lifted his head to look at her, the green eyes dark and troubled.

'No.' Carefully Sophie stood up, hoping her legs wouldn't buckle beneath her.

'Are you uncertain of your feelings?' he tried again. She flushed, shaking her head.

'Then what is it?' Max railed at her impatiently. 'I suppose there is a reason for this—quixotic behaviour?'

'Yes,' she said painfully.

'And you expect to have an affair with me, live with me intimately, sharing mind and body, yet keep this thing from me?' He laughed shortly. 'It's absurd—you must see that.'

He waited for her comment, but she didn't speak.

'And I'd find out what it is sooner or later,' he added grimly.

She clenched her hands.

'It seems I can't give you what you want, and you can't accept what I can give,' she said slowly, her voice low. 'Perhaps we're better apart, not trying something that's doomed to fail before it begins,' she added.

This time he didn't say anything, but his eyes moved away from her to stare into the fire, and she wondered what he was thinking.

'Let's sit down,' he said unexpectedly, 'and see if there's anything we can rescue from all this.'

He moved to a deep armchair and she took a seat opposite, watching him as he leaned back, flexing tired muscles, trying to be rational and keep emotions at bay. He didn't speak, and Sophie thought back over what he had said. She could see what he meant about sharing and entwining their lives if they had an affair. It would be difficult if he wanted marriage and she did not. Slowly her earlier confidence began to fade. Would she be able to keep her secret, or would she be tempted one day to tell him the true reasons she had refused to marry him? And then what would happen? Would he persuade her into marriage and live to regret it later?

Abruptly Max got up. 'There's only one way it could work,' he said coolly. 'If you're prepared to live as my wife, so that everyone believes we're married when in fact we are not.'

She looked up, mystified. 'I don't understand.'

'It's quite simple. We pretend to be married, behave as husband and wife, live in the same house and build a life together. No one need know we've never actually gone through the legal ceremony.'

'It doesn't sound simple. I don't know if I could . . .'

'Those are my terms,' he interrupted shortly. 'If you agree, we remain together and I'll give you my word not to probe your reason for refusing me marriage. Nor would I stand in your way if . . .' he hesitated for a moment, then continued smoothly, '. . . if or when you decided to leave me. I would then be the heartbroken husband in public, instead of the rejected lover. Until, that is, I recovered as I believe all heartbroken husbands invariably do,' he drawled.

Sophie drew a sharp breath.

'I don't understand Max. It's crazy. And why? What would you get out of it?'

He didn't reply, merely looking at her, his regard steady, his face impassive.

'Very well,' she said evenly, 'if you're serious, I'll think about it.'

'You won't. You'll decide now. That at least you owe me. I leave in the morning. It has to be settled tonight.' He laughed shortly. 'It's usually the other way round, isn't it? The woman desperate for marriage, the man reluctant or unwilling? Who knows, there might be some amusement in a reversal of roles. Certainly it has possibilities, wouldn't you say?' His voice hardened. 'I mean it, Sophie. Either you agree to what I propose, or I'll walk out of here tomorrow and we will not meet again.'

'That's blackmail,' she protested angrily.

'So it is,' Max smiled pleasantly.

She stood up and walked away from him. Could she do what he asked, be his wife in public with all the commitment involved, knowing she was merely his mistress? And why did he ask it of her? Had he a more devious plan in mind, something he hadn't yet told her, that she would know once she had committed herself to his charade?

It was all so fraught, the kind of thing that worked in fiction—but not in real life. And she wasn't at all sure she could sustain such a masquerade, she thought miserably. It would mean acting a life of lies and half truths with everyone she met. And he had told her nothing of his family. Were there brothers, sisters, parents to be deceived? The thought of so much deception was oddly distasteful. And what effect would it have on him, on their relationship? How soon would it lead to mistrust of each other?

Yet what was the alternative? And did she have the strength to leave him in the morning never to see him again? She trembled at the thought, her body suddenly cold in the warm room. How could she turn her back on the kind of happiness Max was offering? Without him the rest of her life stretched before her, arid and meaningless. But would he carry out his threat, ensure they didn't meet again, cutting her out of his life?

'Doubts, my Sophie?' he asked quietly behind her.

'Yes,' she said without turning round. 'I don't know if I can live . . . a lie, deceiving people . . .' Her voice broke.

'There's always a price to pay, isn't there?'

'But it's not necessary.' She turned to him, her eyes pleading, her voice low. 'Why can't we just have an affair and . . .'

'No.' He was adamant. 'You would be well provided for,' he said deliberately. 'While we're together—and afterwards.'

'I wouldn't touch your money,' she said sharply.

'You wouldn't?' he mocked her. 'Now, I wonder why?'

'I'd have to tell my sister the truth,' she said gruffly.

'No, Sophie, no exceptions.' He put his hands on her shoulders and looked down into her face. 'Would you believe there are women who would quite like to marry me and spend my money?' he asked softly.

'Then why don't you go to them?' she snapped angrily, her eyes flashing. 'Why bother with me?'

'Why indeed?' he asked, his voice silky as he pulled her into his arms. She stood rigid in his embrace, her head up, her eyes challenging him. 'Whatever it is that's eating you up, my Sophie, we'll sort it out. I never let anything put me off what I want.'

It was hopeless, she thought miserably as he bent his head to kiss her, his hands moving down her back inside the dressing gown till she shivered with longing and responded wildly, winding her arms round his neck and curving her body to his. His mouth crushed hers as they clung to each other and she arched back her head, opening her mouth to his. Finally he released her, unwinding her arms from his neck, his breathing harsh, the dark colour in his face. He was as aroused as she herself.

Looking at his tall back as he turned away, she knew she faced an impossible choice, and if she left him now she would deny herself any chance of happiness. And there was no reason to refuse what he suggested. They were both adult, free to make decisions and abide by the consequences.

Only there was more to it, and Sophie wished passionately that she could ignore the inner voice that was driving her. Max was human. He would continue to speculate about her refusal to marry him. And gradually he would come to resent her secrecy. Then he would turn away from her in bitterness and disappointment until only hatred and mistrust remained. And she knew, even before it had began that their relationship would head for disaster.

The answer stared her in the face, and she wished she could close her mind to it, bury her doubts and throw herself into his arms. But she couldn't.

Slowly she turned round to face him.

CHAPTER SEVEN

SOPHIE locked the front door of her flat and made her way down the short flight of steps to the street. It was cold, but the rain had stopped and she decided to walk to the underground station.

Even after three weeks back home, she found it difficult to forget the cold, crisp sunlight of Kitzbühl. On her return she had abandoned all thought of a holiday, spending her first week sitting miserably in her flat, unable to eat or sleep, missing Max more than she had ever thought possible. Over and over she had remembered every word he'd spoken to her, reliving each moment they'd spent together. In the end she decided to go to the Carringtons' a week early. Work was the best antidote for what ailed her.

Now she shook her head briefly to clear it of emotion. The day had been good, she told herself firmly. She had treated herself to breakfast out and then wandered round the Knightsbridge shops. She loved the area with its bustling streams of people from all over the world, its glittering shops and fabulous restaurants. Mid-morning, the rain had driven her home and she'd made a snack which she ate to the sound of her favourite Léhar operetta. The tiny flat in one of Earls Court's unmodernised backwaters was usually a haven she enjoyed. But restlessness had driven her out, and she had spent the afternoon in the Victoria and Albert Museum.

In Eaton Square the footman let her into the Carrington house.

'Good evening, George,' she said pleasantly, the warmth of the central heating oppressive after the freshness outside.

'The mistress wants you to collect Miss Lisa when you get back,' he informed her, and jerked his head towards the double doors at the back of the hall. 'Company again tonight.'

Sophie nodded and headed for the stairs. In the nursery wing all was quiet. The new baby was still in the care of the nurse who had brought her home from the clinic where she was born, and it would be another month before Sophie took over the care of both children.

The guests were having pre-dinner drinks when Sophie edged her way into the large reception room where Lisa was sitting on her father's knee.

'Good evening, Nanny,' Mr Carrington greeted her, and turned to his daughter. 'Time for bed, poppet.'

Lisa was four years old and very lovely, with curly fair hair and large brown eyes. Because of an early childhood beset with illness, she had been spoiled and become wilful.

'Not yet, Daddy,' she entreated her father, turning imploring eyes up at him. 'I'm not tired—please, can I stay just a bit?' But he was not the parent who spoiled her.

'No, love, it's late. Say goodnight to Mummy and then up to bed with you.'

Lisa pouted, but recognised the firm note in her father's voice and danced away from him across the room to her mother.

'Do I have to go, Mummy?' She tugged at her mother's sleeve. 'Please can I stay?'

There was no doubt where Lisa got her looks. Mrs

Carrington was a real beauty, slim and striking with a face that turned all heads.

'Darling, don't do that.' She pulled the silky material out of the little hand.

'Please, Mummy!' the child tried again.

'If you're going to be naughty, you won't be able to come down again,' her mother warned absently, her attention with her guests.

To Sophie this was a familiar scene, and she knew it could not be resolved with patience. Bending down to the little girl, she picked her up, holding her firmly as Lisa began to wriggle.

'No!' Lisa protested, not sure if she was angry or upset. 'I hate you, let me go!' she whispered vehemently, and pummelled Sophie with her fists. Taking no notice of the guests round her, Sophie forged through the centre of the room to the door. Before she could put out a hand to open it, someone was there before her.

'Thank you,' she murmured politely as the man stepped back, holding the door for her. Fleetingly she threw him a glance over her shoulder to give him a formal smile. And then she stopped in frozen disbelief.

Max!

He was regarding her gravely, his face unsmiling as she gripped the child too tightly and Lisa began to cry in earnest. For a moment Sophie couldn't move, her muscles refusing to obey her brain. Then he came forward as if to help her and she sprang to life, almost rushing away from him out into the hall, her mind a blank, her body moving automatically.

It wasn't possible. How could he be here? He'd sworn never to try and see her again. What could he want?

As she went through the familiar routine of putting
the child to bed and reading a familiar story till Lisa
calmed down, Sophie's mind was leaping about.
When she finally turned out the light on the sleeping
child, she trailed wearily to her own room and sank
into a chair. Staring blankly at nothing, she sat on,
heedless of the time or the meal waiting for her that
would be long cold.

It was the shock of seeing him so unexpectedly that
had unnerved her downstairs, bringing a sudden
panic that she couldn't control. But now she
wondered why he was here. Was he merely a guest,
unaware of her presence in the house? Or had he
come to find her? Her pulses hammered at the
thought. Had he missed her, she thought with
yearning, and changed his mind about their having
an affair? Sophie's throat tightened. Perhaps ...

A knock brought her out of her chair. It was George
still on duty; when their employers entertained, the
staff worked late.

'It's the master,' he whispered, mindful not to
wake the child. 'He would be glad if you could come
down to the study.'

'Now?' Sophie asked in astonishment.

'Yes.'

In the study Mr Carrington was not alone. Max
stood across the room, regarding her intently, and she
turned her head away, fighting the elation she felt at
the sight of him.

'I must apologise for disturbing you so late,' said
Mr Carrington smoothly. 'Won't you sit down?'

'I think I'll stand, thank you,' she said quietly, and
waited.

He was a nice man. Slim and short, grey hair
receding from a domed forehead, he looked, as

always, impeccably groomed. The gossip in the servants' hall was that he had been disappointed at the birth of a second daughter, that he had badly wanted a son. But Sophie had seen no sign of displeasure in his treatment of the baby on his daily visits to the nursery. As he smiled at her with kindness she guessed that he was probably a very good diplomat indeed.

'I understand you're acquainted with Baron von Hartog, so there is no need to introduce him to you,' he said quietly. 'He has asked me if he might have a few moments' private conversation with you, and I've explained that I cannot permit you to be embarrassed in any way. If you're prepared to hear what he has to say, that is a private matter between you. But if you don't wish for this conversation, I shall not hesitate to refuse his request.'

Sophie didn't answer immediately. Her first instinct was to refuse. Had Max changed his mind and now wanted an affair with her, he could have written or even phoned. This request for an immediate meeting, here in the house where she was employed, upset her. She didn't want to talk to him ... alone, afraid of what would happen, what he could do to her. Already she could feel the tension from him across the room, pounding at her pulses, confusing her senses as she responded to his presence. But would he accept a refusal? Or would he try again to see her until she gave in? Perhaps it would be better to deal with whatever he wanted—now.

Mr Carrington was watching the thoughts cross her face, but made no move to hurry her.

'Very well,' she said at last, and walked away from them both.

'I'll leave you, then,' he said behind her. 'No doubt

we'll see you in a few minutes, Max.'

Max. So the two men were on Christian name terms. She heard a low thank you from Max before the door closed quietly behind her employer.

'Will you please turn round and look at me, Sophie?'

Slowly she turned, her head up, her breathing tight. He looked magnificent. The black and white of the evening clothes set off the tall, broad figure. His hair gleamed thick and silky in the soft light from the desk lamp, and his skin was darkly tanned as she remembered, his face so achingly familiar that the breath caught in her throat with sudden longing. But something was different. The faint smile on his lips seemed forced, and didn't light up his eyes as she remembered. And he was watching her with a wary, guarded look.

'I'm sorry to intrude on you at this hour,' he began softly. 'I arrived late last night and have been trying to reach you all day. I was told you were on leave and rang your flat, but there was no reply. In the end I went round there, but you were out.'

Her eyes veered from his face. He had been trying to find her.

'What is it you want, Max?' she asked evenly.

'You're mighty cool,' he said sharply, his politeness slipping. 'So where were you today? Out with some man, no doubt?'

'Can we please get on with whatever you want of me?' she said, veiling her eyes. Her heart was thudding in the old familiar way, and she was afraid he would see how much he disturbed her.

'I'm not here on my own account,' he said more quietly. 'I bring a message from my grandmother. She wishes to meet you.'

'Your grandmother?' Sophie echoed stupidly. 'But how——' She broke off. 'Why would she want to meet me?'

He moved to stare down into the fire. 'I've told her about you: how we met, that I fell in love with you and asked you to marry me, that you turned me down.'

'But ... I ... why did you tell her all that?' she stammered.

'We're close,' he said tautly. 'She knows me well and guessed most of it anyway.' He clenched one hand on the mantelpiece. 'One way and another the past three weeks haven't been exactly easy for me. Obviously it's been quite different for you,' he added harshly.

Again she turned away from him. Her composure was shaken. Max had not come because he'd missed her and wanted to change his mind, accept her offer of an affair. She clenched her hands. Nothing had changed, and she had to be rational, to keep her feelings rigidly under control.

'If you told her about us,' she went on more steadily, 'she must know we don't see each other any more.'

He sighed and straightened up. 'Yes, I've told her. But she still wants to meet you. And she's used to getting her own way because I love her and because she's old.' His voice hardened. 'I want you to agree to this meeting, Sophie.'

'But, Max, be reasonable. We could have nothing to talk about, and I ...'

'For God's sake don't be so crassly selfish!' he interrupted angrily. 'Can't you ever think of anyone but yourself?'

She bit hard on her lower lip to stop the angry

words she wanted to hurl at him. He had no right to upbraid her ... or to dictate to her. Perhaps it would be easier to agree to a meeting with his grandmother and then slide out of it politely when the time came. In his present mood it was pointless to argue with him.

'Very well, Max, I will do as you ask. Where do I go for this meeting?'

'My home in Salzburg.'

'Austria?' Her voice rose in astonishment. 'You expect me to travel to Austria to see her?'

'That's where she lives.'

'But that's impossible. I couldn't possibly ...'

'For heaven's sake, don't make such a production out of it. A few days, a week at the most—that's all it would be. She's threatened to come to London if you don't agree. And that would be against the strongest advice of her doctors.' He paced the room in short angry strides. 'Have you so little human feeling that you can refuse such a simple request?' He hesitated. 'I tried to dissuade her,' he went on grimly, 'but she's adamant.'

'But why, Max, what does she want of me?'

He shrugged. 'God knows. A whim? Curiosity to see who's finally brought me to my knees?' he drawled watching the colour flush her face. 'Who can say what motivates a woman?' He walked over to the desk and stood with his back to her, his hands thrust deep into his trouser pockets. 'Even you can't be so ruthlessly selfish as to deny an old woman what she wants so badly,' he added coldly.

He sounded so bitter, Sophie thought unhappily. Obviously he regretted his feelings for her, and she could hardly blame him. Was this meeting with his grandmother to be a sort of test? Did he hope she would show up badly in the grandeur of his home, and free him from a love that tied him to her against his will? She shivered with trepidation. It would be madness to go. She would have to watch him living the life she might have shared with him in the home of which she might have been the mistress. Whatever his grandmother might want of her, such a meeting could only lead to more heartache, a second parting from Max harder to bear than the first.

Unexpectedly he whirled round and came towards her. Before she could back away, he had gripped her shoulders.

'You don't care, do you?' he ground out. 'Nothing matters to you except your own convenience. How you hurt others is of no interest.'

She stared at him in consternation. He was in a white rage, his eyes flashing, his lips thinned, the pain he inflicted with his fingers bringing tears to her eyes.

'Then you must be pleased to be rid of me,' she managed, her head up.

'Oh, I am,' he sneered. 'I damn well am. Relieved and thankful,' he muttered, and bent to kiss her, catching her half-parted lips in an angry assault. There was no tenderness or passion in his kiss. It was a punishment, and Sophie felt her lips crack as his teeth grazed her skin. She hated him for what he was doing, but felt her body respond to his touch as he plundered her mouth, her head arched back under the pressure.

At last he lifted his head and released her.

'Dear God, Sophie, just say you'll come. Don't refuse me again.'

'I didn't refuse you,' she said sadly. 'I wanted only to be with you, but I couldn't accept your conditions.' She raised her head and looked up into his face. Her voice when it came was strangled and almost inaudible. 'I can't do as you ask, Max. Please apologise to your grandmother for me.'

The narrow staircase was dark as Sophie pushed open the front door. Upstairs the outer office was empty. Lottie's secretary didn't work on Saturdays.

'Anyone in?' Sophie called, and the inner door opened.

'There you are.' Lottie appeared in the doorway.

Inside her office it was suffocatingly hot, a wall gas fire going full blast, all the windows tightly shut. Sophie took off her coat.

'Close the door, there's a good girl.' Lottie shivered. 'Terrible draught.' She sat down behind her desk and picked up a half-smoked cigarette from a giant glass ash-tray. 'There's some coffee. Help yourself.'

'Coffee?' said Sophie brightly. 'This is an honour.' She poured the thick black liquid into the mug.

'There's no milk, but plenty of sugar.' Lottie leaned back in her chair. 'Talking of honour, to what do I owe this visit? On your free day, too.'

Sophie sat down, not really sure why she'd come. It was almost a week since Max's visit, and she had been trying ever since to put him out of her mind. By Thursday her head had begun to clear, the ache round her heart slightly dulled. And then the invitation arrived. A thick cream card, embossed with the von Hartog crest, it had confirmed the invitation from Max's grandmother, suggesting a date for the visit.

'I just thought I'd say hello,' she said rather vaguely.

'Really?' Lottie was sceptical. 'It wouldn't have

anything to do with the appearance of Max von Hartog in London, would it?'

Sophie felt the blush rise from her neck and looked intently down at her coffee. 'How do you know about that?'

'He came to see me.'

'To see you?' Sophie looked up.

'Of course. How do you imagine he knew where to find you?'

'I thought he knew the Carringtons.'

'I expect he did. At a rough guess I'd say he probably made their acquaintance about two hours after he left me.' Lottie laughed at Sophie's astonishment. 'He wouldn't have had any difficulty introducing himself. He's quite a distinguished figure in Vienna, after all. And Carrington moves to his new posting there in the autumn.' Sophie looked puzzled. 'He's going to the Vienna embassy.'

'Oh.' Sophie frowned. 'I wouldn't have to go with them, would I?'

'Your contract is the usual one for a year. And your speaking German was a big plus when I negotiated your salary.'

'Oh.'

'Why don't you tell me about it?' Lottie suggested, and got up to pour herself more coffee. Sophie didn't answer. 'Look—it's your life, love, and if you don't want to talk about it I certainly won't probe.' She came back and sat down. 'But I'm not quite the old fool you seem to think me. I can still recognise a man head over heels in love.'

'It's all over,' said Sophie tonelessly.

'Not for him, it isn't.' Lottie paused. 'What is it, Sophie? Did he want an affair and you refused?'

'No,' Sophie replied miserably. 'I wanted an affair. He wanted marriage.'

'Good grief,' Lottie said after a stunned moment. 'I must be getting old—or going crazy. You refused to marry him?'

'I don't want to talk about it,' said Sophie dully. 'I came about this.' She pushed the invitation across the table.

Lottie put on her glasses and read it in silence.

'And how can I help you with this?'

'I thought—well, you know the family. How can I refuse so that I don't hear from her again?'

Lottie raised her eyebrows. 'In my day one sent a polite refusal and regrets. What's so difficult?'

'I have refused, but she won't take no for an answer.'

'I wonder why?' asked Lottie thoughtfully.

'She's used to having her own way.' Sophie put down her mug and looked pleadingly at the older woman. 'Would you answer it for me? Tell her I've gone away and won't be back for a while. You'll know just what to say.'

It was Lottie's turn to stare in surprise. 'And could you please explain to me why I should tell a lot of lies to protect you from an old woman?'

Sophie didn't answer. She was miserably conscious that this visit had turned out to be another mistake. Nothing seemed to be going right at the moment.

'Never mind,' she said, and got up. 'Thanks, anyway.'

'Why don't you try telling him the truth?' Lottie asked quietly. Sophie stiffened and turned away.

'I do know, Sophie. I've always known,' she added softly.

'No,' Sophie whispered ashen-faced. 'Nobody knows.'

'Come and sit down again another minute,' said Lottie gently.

Sophie subsided on to the hard chair as Lottie got up and stood by the window, her eyes on Sophie's face.

'When you first came to me I contacted your parents, as I do with any new girl. They told me some of it, and for the rest I approached the convent.' She hesitated. 'I've often wondered why you didn't realise I had to know. I did get you your first passport, and for that I needed a birth certificate.'

'You never mentioned it,' Sophie said tonelessly.

'It wasn't important to me. "Father unknown", the birth certificate read. That means you're probably illegitimate. Since your mother died only hours after you were born, we'll never know.' Lottie hesitated. 'There are millions of girls out there in the same predicament, you know,' she added softly. 'It's hardly a tragedy in this day and age.'

Sophie didn't say anything, her eyes lowered to her bag which she found she was clutching tightly between her fingers.

'You haven't told him, have you?'

Sophie shook her head.

'Are you ashamed of it?'

'Not really,' Sophie said slowly. 'It all happened before I was born. I suppose I feel a bit . . . incomplete. It's not easy to explain.'

'But it's not as if you were abandoned and institutionalised. You were adopted before you were a year old. You have a name, a family and parents who brought you up.'

'I know,' agreed Sophie huskily. 'I was one of the lucky ones.'

'Did you ever go back to the convent to try and trace your family?'

'Yes.'

'And what did you find out?'

'The nuns were very helpful and told me all they knew. But they knew nothing of my parentage, and there was no way I could trace my family. In most ways it was a dead end,' she added, flushing.

'And why didn't you tell your Maximilian?'

'He's not mine,' Sophie insisted stubbornly. 'I did think about it,' she admitted, 'but I decided against it.'

'Why?'

'I think he would have married me in spite of it,' she said painfully, 'and perhaps it wouldn't have mattered right away. But after a while he would have wondered. His friends and family would have been ... curious. And it's not as if he's just anybody. He has a position to keep up, a famous name to consider.' She swallowed hard. 'And he has to have a son to follow after him,' she added softly.

'So? Don't tell me you don't want children of your own?'

'I ... I can't have children,' Sophie said in a rush.

'Rubbish. You know that's nonsense. You were completely checked out before I took you on.'

'It's not exactly that I'm physically incapable.' She raised her head. 'You don't know about that?'

Lottie shook her head. 'So tell me.'

'I don't really want to talk about it.'

'And you're quite sure about this ... whatever it is ... impediment.'

'Quite sure,' said Sophie firmly.

Lottie sighed and came back to sit down.

'Well,' she said eventually, 'you came to me for help, and for what it's worth, here it is. I advise you to be honest with your Max. He's not a child that needs protection. He's a grown man who can make his own decisions.' She sat up straight and looked directly into Sophie's eyes. 'I think you're running scared. You don't dare tell him the truth about yourself because you might find out he doesn't love you enough to overlook the circumstances of your birth. And that would be painful.' She hesitated. 'But at least it would clear up all misunderstandings, and if he turned his back on you, however painful that would be, you could then put the whole thing behind you and make a new life for yourself—or go back to the one you have—with a clear head and unclouded emotions. But leaving him in the dark, and remaining unsure of the strength of his feelings for you, you will find the whole thing will always haunt you. And you'll always look back and wonder, what if I'd told him . . .? And that could sour your whole life because nothing would ever measure up to the dreams of him you didn't dare put to the test.'

Sophie sat very still, her eyes on Lottie's face, listening intently to everything she said.

'So go to him . . . visit his grandmother. Stop crouching behind your fears. And if the opportunity arises, tell him about yourself—everything. Whatever the outcome, you'll be better able to live with yourself afterwards.'

She got up. 'And now I'm going to throw you out. You may have all day, but I have work to do. Let me know what you decide,' she added gruffly. 'And the Carringtons you can leave to me. I'll work something out.'

CHAPTER EIGHT

'FASTEN Seatbelts.'

The sign flashed on above her head and Sophie sighed with relief as the plane began its descent to Salzburg airport.

The journey had seemed endless. The last two days in London had been too busy to give her time to think or speculate. But once strapped in her seat on the plane, there was suddenly nothing more to do, and her thoughts rambled in disjointed confusion, as they always did at times of uncertainty.

Should she be going to Austria? she wondered once more. Had she made the right decision, or had she allowed Lottie to persuade her against her better judgment? Still she wasn't sure, and was apprehensive of what faced her at her destination.

'Fräulein Carter?' The uniformed chauffeur approached her as she emerged from customs.

She nodded, and he took her suitcase before ushering her out into the cold where a large limousine was waiting at the kerb. Seated in the back of the luxuriously appointed car, she found her eyes drawn to the yellow and gold flag fluttering on the bonnet, and her mind became numbed with foreboding. The countryside they passed blurred as she gazed blindly out at the snow.

Leaving the ring road that circled the town, they climbed steadily, passing through several villages, till they entered into deep woods. Here the road narrowed, the snow packed high on both sides, hiding the valley below from view. As they emerged from the trees, Sophie caught a glimpse of the arrowed signpost. Schloss Hartog.

Nervously she gripped her handbag and sat forward on the edge of the seat as the chauffeur swung the car sharply into a private road and headed towards tall iron gates standing open at the far end.

The driveway beyond was short and lined with slim, high cypresses that towered darkly above them. They emerged on to a wide expanse of gravel, and Sophie had her first sight of Max's home.

Until that moment her mind had been vaguely filled with pictures of castles from childhood fairy tales: thick walls and narrow slit windows, huge towers and winding staircases giving access to small, dark rooms. The reality before her was stunningly different.

Set in a clearing free from the surrounding trees, the castle rose in majestic splendour, its baroque façade wide and elegant, its colour in the glow of the afternoon sun a dazzling yellow gold. Not a fairytale castle, but a private palace from the eighteenth century.

Large windows ran the length of each of its four stories, the symmetry broken only by a centre balcony, stone-railed and jutting from the first floor to form an arched roof for the main entrance below.

The surrounding gardens were deeply buried in snow; clipped yew hedges were just visible along the terraces where Sophie glimpsed two giant carriage lamps, their thick stone feet embedded in the squat pillars on which they perched, their sloping iron and glass frames clear of snow. On the far side, extensive woods hid the castle from the main road, wide paths stretching away under thick fir trees that rose to top the roof of the castle.

As the car drove under the archway and stopped before the heavily studded iron door, Sophie sat bemused, stunned by the beauty of the castle and its setting. Inside, the inner door gave on to a panelled hall, where modern sofas and comfortable chairs were grouped round a roaring log fire, windows at the far end giving a glorious view across the gardens and the woods beyond. A woman was waiting to greet her.

'Frau Glaser,' she introduced herself in German. 'I am the housekeeper and welcome you to Schloss Hartog. The Frau Baron asked me to give you her apologies for not greeting you in person. She hopes you will join her for tea when you have rested.'

'Thank you,' Sophie smiled, just as a low growl from behind had her spinning round to see an enormous black dog raise himself from the hearth and move deliberately towards her.

She froze. He looked dangerous and distinctly hostile.

'Here, Boy,' a familiar voice said behind her, and she turned to see Max von Hartog in the doorway. The dog changed direction, and Max leaned down to touch one hand to his collar while he murmured to him softly. Without lifting his head he spoke.

'Just walk towards me, Sophie, quite slowly.' She obeyed instinctively. 'Give me your hand,' he said when she reached him, and a slight quiver shook her at the touch of those firm warm fingers. He placed her hand on the dog's collar, resting it against the powerful neck. 'Say something,' he instructed, 'anything, just to let him hear your voice.'

'Hello,' she said softly, and stroked the short silky hair. 'You are a beauty, aren't you?'

The dog arched his neck and looked up at her. He was truly magnificent. A beautiful wide forehead, white touched with brown, long black ears and a proud lift to the head; intelligent dark eyes now gazed at Sophie with a hard unblinking stare.

'He's a Rottweiler,' Max explained. 'Like the St Bernard dogs, the Rottweilers go back to the Middle Ages when they were highly prized as cattle dogs. Now they're used mainly in police work, because they're quiet, very intelligent and enormously courageous.' He straightened up. 'I had Boy as a puppy and trained him to do mountain rescue work with me.' He paused and added softly, 'How I wished for him the day of the avalanche!'

Hurriedly Sophie turned her head away as she felt the colour rise from her neck.

'But he's dangerous,' Max went on. 'He kills without compunction.' She gasped, and he glanced round at her shocked face. 'You've no need to fear him,' he assured her. 'He's accepted you.'

Her heart was pounding, standing so close to him and listening to his words. He was wearing the traditional Austrian costume, the slim grey trousers with brown wooden buttons and green braiding on the smooth wool of the jacket. On other men Sophie had always considered it too theatrical, as though designed for a musical comedy. But on Max it looked right, casually elegant in the way it fitted across the wide shoulders and fell to his narrow hips.

As though aware of her scrutiny, he turned his head to look at her. She did not flinch, meeting those clear green eyes with a steady regard. And then her breath caught in her throat. The eyes were empty. Bland and expressionless, they were regarding her with disinterested friendliness. In London there had been tension and anger. Emotion had flared and been quickly controlled. But she could find no feeling at all in that curiously blank stare.

Slowly, and with unexpected force, a tight pain seemed to constrict her heart as the hopes she had secretly cherished crumbled and died. Max no longer cared for her. Perhaps Lottie had been wrong, or perhaps his interest had finished in London. His indifference was clearly genuine. She began to shiver, and held herself rigidly to control it. He must not guess at her distress.

'You'll want to rest now,' he said, and released the dog. 'Frau Glaser will show you your room. My grandmother takes tea at four-thirty. Perhaps you could be ready then.'

Sophie was ready and waiting when the knock sounded on her door an hour later. She had bathed and changed into a wool skirt and matching sweater, adding a brilliant green silk scarf to contrast with the soft tobacco-brown of her outfit.

'You had a good flight?' Max asked politely as they walked along the corridor.

'Thank you, yes,' she said, and lapsed into silence.

She was flustered and too preoccupied with her own feelings to take note of her surroundings. Acutely aware of Max and his long fluid stride at her side, she wondered what lay ahead. Until this moment she had not given any thought to what his grandmother might actually want from her.

On the floor below, an elderly woman opened the door to Max's knock. Sturdily built, she had grey hair braided round her head; her pale face was clear of make-up, her brown eyes oddly hostile.

'Hello, Martha. My grandmother up?' asked Max

in German, and Sophie wondered who she was. A maid? A companion? Max didn't introduce them.

The sitting-room beyond the hallway was high-ceilinged but surprisingly cosy, with satin curtains at the windows, an open fire and several thick Turkish carpets on the parquet floor. A round mahogany table was surrounded by velvet-upholstered chairs, and several china lamps with pearl-fringed knotted shades stood round the room on occasional tables. The tapestry-lined walls were in muted shades of grey, an inlaid side table covered with photographs in silver frames of all shapes and sizes.

'*Grand'mère*.' Max moved across the room as an old lady came through a door at the far end. He bent his head to kiss her cheek, and led her to a chair where she settled herself.

'Don't fuss, Max,' she said in German as he hovered and raised her head to look at Sophie still standing inside the door.

'This is Sophie Carter, *Grand'mère*,' Max said formally, one hand protectively on his grandmother's shoulder. 'My grandmother, Frau Baron Véronique von Hartog.'

Sophie nodded and tried to smile, but her face felt stiff and rigid.

'Come and sit down,' the old lady said in heavily accented English before she looked up at her grandson. 'Thank you, Max, I don't believe we'll need you now.'

He took her hand and bent to kiss it.

'Yes, yes,' she complained, 'there's no need to overdo it.' But she softened the remark by reaching out to caress his cheek lightly with one small hand, her eyes tender on his bent head.

A lump rose in Sophie's throat. They're very close,

she thought with sudden envy, sensing the deep understanding between them.

'Sophie.' He bowed politely and she looked up to catch the cool indifference in his glance. The next moment he had gone.

'Tea, I think, Martha,' her hostess ordered, and watched the other woman leave. 'I have to thank you for coming,' she said formally, 'and at considerable inconvenience.'

Sophie lifted her head to find herself being carefully scrutinised. Deliberately she had worn a simple outfit, making no effort to try and appear glamorous. But now she felt self-conscious, and for the first time for many years she wished passionately that she had the looks and wealth to dazzle this woman. The inspection continued, steady eyes probing with a curious intensity, and finally Sophie rallied, looking back at the other woman with equal curiosity.

Had she been asked what she had expected Max's grandmother to be, she would have replied without hesitation: a frail old lady. Instead she was confronted by an indomitable aristocrat. From the top of her white, softly styled hair to the high-heeled buttoned boots, she was unmistakably a lady of the old order. Sitting very straight, her waist tightly corseted, she wore her afternoon tea gown with true elegance, a gold brooch at her throat, a long rope of even-sized pearls hanging to her waist and a large emerald ring on her right hand. The heavy-lidded eyes were as green as her grandson's and her soft skin was pale and wrinkled. Not beautiful, but a face of strength and character.

Why had she wanted this meeting? What could she

possibly hope to gain from it? Her face gave Sophie no clue.

'You speak French?' the Frau Baron asked unexpectedly.

'A little.'

'Me, I am French. The German I détest. It rumbles and has no lightness, no sophistication. My grandson—he has a passion for the English.'

'I will try to follow your French,' offered Sophie.

'No.' She thought for a moment. 'We try the English. And if I mistake, you do not scold, *n'est-ce pas*?'

Sophie smiled.

'Ah, when you smile, your face—*ça change*!' She put her head on one side. 'It has the animation.' She paused. 'But beautiful you are not,' she added sadly.

Faintly Sophie blushed. 'No,' she agreed shortly.

'So why, I ask myself, has my beauty-loving grandson chosen you?' She was genuinely perplexed. 'More than ten years I wait. *Mon Dieu*, how I wait—for the marriage, the children. And the women they come and they go. Some love him, some do not.' She shrugged. 'He has money, a title and a handsome face. For most women it is enough. They ask no more. But always for him it is—*pas sérieux*. You understand?'

Sophie nodded. The old lady was a real charmer, her small hands emphasising her words, expressions chasing across her face which lifted and shed years as she talked vivaciously.

'Not this one, *Grand'mère*, he says. Not yet, he says. Be patient. But patience I have had too long.' Her hands stilled and she gripped the arms of her chair, looking directly into Sophie's eyes. 'And now there is you. And for me the waiting is at an end. But you say no. You refuse the marriage. And I want to meet you, to see the woman who can say no to my Max. It is to me *incroyable*—impossible!'

There was silence when she finished, and Sophie looked down at her clasped hands, curiously at a loss how to deal with this fascinating woman.

'I do not frighten you into excuses,' the older woman went on after a moment. 'Perhaps I begin to see how he might love you—the quiet, the strength. Will you tell me now why you do not wish to marry him?'

Sophie looked up just as the door opened and Martha appeared with tea. She was relieved at the interruption and watched the two women busy with sugar and lemon, cake and biscuits.

'I, too, am obstinate,' the Frau Baron went on as she settled with her cup and Martha left them to sit unobtrusively in a corner with some sewing.

'Obstinate?'

'*Oui*. I think you are. When you make up the mind, you do not change it, I think.'

'Perhaps', Sophie admitted with a small smile.

'So it is not possible to—how you say—jump into confidence with you?' The old lady stirred her tea, but her lively eyes were on Sophie, searching for reactions. 'We must hope my grandson can persuade you to change that mind.' She smiled broadly. 'If I were betting, it would be on him,' she added, pleased with her own words. 'For the moment you and I will get to know each other.'

Dressing for dinner, Sophie thought back to that short exchange. It seemed Véronique von Hartog had hoped for a beautiful wife for her grandson, but was prepared to settle for what she thought he wanted. She wished Max had told his grandmother exactly what had happened between them in Kitzbühl. That would have avoided misunderstandings and disappointments. That she had rather liked the old lady at their meeting today only added to existing complications.

Absently she looked at her clothes. Before leaving London she had bought two new evening dresses, and she now pulled out the less formal. Hand-sewn in heavy silk jersey with long sleeves and lowered waistline, the dress was a deep rich blue, a striking contrast to the darkness of her hair; the full skirt was flattering to her long legs. Checking her appearance in the full-length mirror, she was conscious of the vanity that had prompted her to buy a dress she couldn't really afford and would have no occasion to wear again. In the expensive London boutique, all she had wanted was for Max to see her wearing it. Only it had been a pointless extravagance. Whatever his grandmother believed, Sophie was convinced of his indifference.

The family dining-room was a surprise. It was neither formal or grand as she had expected. The oval table with its white damask, cut glass and monogrammed silver occupied the centre of the room, graceful rococo chairs grouped round it. In one corner stood a slender ceramic stove, its shimmering lilac colour echoing the faint blue threads in the embroidered tapestries that hung on the walls. Darkened windows, their inside shutters folded back, reflected the lights from a gilded chandelier suspended over the table, and more lights flickered from tall yellow candles at the side of two scrolled baroque mirrors.

As she sat opposite Max, his grandmother between them, the image of the room stared back at Sophie, the three people at the table hazy and insubstantial as a mirage. Max had changed into a dark blue velvet smoking jacket worn with black trousers and a white frilled shirt. He had barely glanced at her as she appeared, his attention on the wine he was pouring into long-stemmed fluted glasses.

A clear vegetable consommé was followed by fillets of sole served with tiny french beans, and Sophie realised that she was hungry. The conversation at table between Max and his grandmother was desultory while the servants came and went. It was not until fruit, coffee and cheese appeared that the servants left them.

'Well, my dear, tomorrow we must plan how to make the most of your stay,' Véronique von Hartog said as she peeled a pear. 'Perhaps we should start with a tour of the plantation, Max. What do you think?'

He looked startled. 'Of course, if Sophie wishes, but there's not really all that much to see. I'm afraid she might be bored.'

'Nonsense. You always take visitors from England to the forests, and they all love it.'

He nodded his agreement. 'It can be arranged whenever convenient.'

'Please,' Sophie intervened. 'I don't wish to cause problems. I'm not here as a tourist, after all. I hope to spend my time with you, *madame*.'

'And so you shall. We'll have coffee together in the morning. Then we can plan. I love planning,' she said grandly.

'I'd like that.'

'And now, Max, please ring the bell for Martha. It's time I retired.'

'May I help you upstairs?'

'No, thank you, my dear. Martha knows just what to do and I wouldn't dream of taking you away from your coffee.'

Sophie said no more, but she noticed the sudden pallor in the old lady's face and wondered if she was in pain. Martha appeared, and Max helped his grandmother to the door, kissing her goodnight.

'*Bonne nuit, mes enfants,*' she said with a smile.

Max came back into the room. 'A liqueur?' he asked.

'Not for me, thanks.' Sophie was nervously anxious to be gone. 'I'm rather tired myself. I had an early start this morning. I think I'll follow your grandmother's example and go up to bed.' She rose from the table.

'There's no need to panic,' he drawled. 'I'm not about to pounce on you.'

The colour surged into her face. 'I never imagined you would,' she snapped at him, angry at his presumption.

'Then there's no reason to run away, is there?' he said coolly.

She hesitated, searching for an excuse to leave. He reached for a cigar from a small smoking table and held it up. 'Do you mind?'

She shook her head, and watched him as he lowered his eyes to the flame of the lighter. In the stylish evening clothes, with the candlelight flickering across the handsome face, he seemed suddenly the embodiment of everything in her life that had always been out of reach. How could she have imagined his feelings were more than transitory infatuation? He loved beauty. His grandmother had said so, and she could see evidence of it all round her. With his looks and his heritage he could choose a wife from among the beauties of Europe, a woman from his own familiar world, of impeccable lineage, able to run his home and bear his children. She herself had no place here—as wife or mistress. And she had been a fool, a naïve idiot to listen to Lottie. Whatever had been between them was over. And all she felt now was embarrassment that she was here at all, an intruder pushing herself unasked into his life.

Max looked up and caught her eyes on him.

'Why are you here, Sophie?' he asked quietly.

Blindly she turned away. Behind her she heard him move and the next instant he was barring her way, his back to the closed door. She stood still, her head lowered away from him.

'Well?' he demanded softly. 'Do I get an answer?'

'I accepted your grandmother's invitation for a short visit,' she said steadily. 'But I realise now it was a mistake. It would be best if I leave.'

'No.' He reached out to clasp her wrist, his fingers tight on her skin.

'Please. You're hurting me!' He was so close she could hear his breathing and see the flash of anger in his eyes. As she watched, the black of his pupils seemed to enlarge and she looked away from the intensity of his stare. Her legs felt weak and she began to tremble.

Abruptly he released her wrist and reached for her, bending his head to kiss her, a bruising, demanding kiss that opened her lips and thrust savagely into her mouth as he pulled her into the powerful strength of his body. Her head tipped back under the pressure and his lips moved to her throat, swift kisses burning her skin. His hands raked down her back into her waist, his fingers hot and hard through the silk of her dress.

His mouth returned to her face, moving softly along her jaw and up to her eyelids, light caresses that left her aching for more. She was blindingly aware of the desire she was arousing in him and responded instinctively, her arms reaching up to his neck, her lips against the roughness of his jaw. He moved his head to crush her lips under his in a kiss of possession that drained the air from her lungs, his hands reaching down to pull her hard against him, the heated muscles of his body scorching through the barrier of their clothes.

Compulsively they strained towards each other, their mouths clinging hungrily, their hands reaching to explore, starved for the feel and touch of each other.

At last Max lifted his head.

'Tell me you came for this, Sophie,' he demanded roughly. 'Say it!'

She looked up at him bemused, her eyes dazed. His face was hot and running with colour, his eyes feverish. She lifted her lips to his.

'Yes,' she breathed into his mouth.

He pulled her back into his arms and buried his face in the warmth of her neck.

'Not here,' he whispered shakily. 'Will you come with me—trust me?'

She nodded and he lifted her, striding out into the brightly lit corridor. In the lift he let her down and kissed her again, their bodies moulded together as the lift carried them up. Then she was once more in his arms, held easily as he stepped into a dark room and carried her over to a wide bed. She watched him pull back the curtains, letting in the starlit night before he locked the door and came back to the bed, sitting on the edge.

'I want very much to see you without that beautiful dress,' he said softly, 'but first I have to be sure you really want this.' He put out a hand and caressed her cheek with his knuckles. 'Are you sure, Sophie? It's not too late to draw back.'

'I'm sure,' she answered him gravely, her eyes steady on his face. She wanted this passionately, had wanted it all those long, lonely nights in London. Whatever happened, she wouldn't regret being here with him.

Very gently he began to undress her, removing each garment with expertise, his fingers barely brushing her skin, the light touch sending spirals of delight along her nerve ends. When the last of the satin and lace was flung aside, Sophie felt the heat flush her body with sudden shyness as he gazed down at her. Slowly his eyes moved over her, the full, firmly rounded breasts, the slender waist and curved hips, the long legs. And for endless moments he was quite still, his breathing harsh, his eyes gleaming in the dim light, a pulse beating heavily in his throat.

She could see his fingers tremble as he began on his own clothes, tossing away each item until her breath caught hard in her throat at the sight of his magnificent body. Deeply tanned, he looked dark above her, his muscled strength a devastating contrast to her soft weakness. And a shiver of fear touched her. He was a giant of a man, and his power and size seemed suddenly menacing. When he sank down on the bed and she felt the hard warmth of him, she lay stiff and tense at his side.

Then he began to stroke her, touching, lingering and caressing, until excitement rose in her like a tidal wave, taking her unawares and electrifying her senses. She tried to lie still under his hands, but her body twisted and arched at his touch, her mind unable to control the tide of her response, her voice crying out to him impatiently.

'Hush, not so fast, my lovely one,' he whispered huskily. Distantly she heard his voice, and then his mouth came down on hers in a kiss that sent her reeling out of control. Nothing she had ever imagined prepared her for the passion that erupted between them as their bodies entwined and their mouths clung. The last of her fear faded away and her mind drifted on a cloud of feeling, the only reality the hard desire of his body and her own longing for him.

Suddenly his fingers bit sharply into her back. She cried out as he lifted his head to look down into her face.

'Now will you marry me?' he demanded hotly.

Silently Sophie stared at him. Her feelings were at fever pitch and her mind dazed. Max gripped her shoulders and began to shake her.

'Say it,' he demanded jerkily. 'I will marry, you Max. Just five words.'

'But Max . . . I—oh, God, not now!'

'Now,' he said implacably.

'But why?' she asked on a sob. 'What are you trying to do?'

'Just say it.'

'You know I can't.' Her voice was a whisper.

'Do you dare deny it—here in my arms? Do you? Have you the gall to tell me you don't want me and love me?'

She twisted her face away and tried to free herself from his hold, but he tightened his grip.

'But—you know. We've been through all this.' She was crying softly.

'Not like this we haven't. Together in bed.'

She lay quite still, her eyes closed, unable to think.

'Sophie,' he threatened. When she didn't speak, he touched his lips to her ear. 'Shall I tell you what I'll do if you refuse? I'll get up and leave you here, aching for me. And you'll never know what delirium of pleasure we could have had together.'

She bit hard on her lip. Did he mean it? Could he stop now when his desire for her was as strong as her own? So should she tell him now about herself as Lottie had suggested? No. She couldn't do it. Not here and now. And yet hadn't she come precisely for this? When she accepted his grandmother's invitation, hadn't she decided then that he should know the truth?

Max rolled away from her.

'I see,' he said grimly, and got out of bed, picking up a robe and shrugging himself into it. 'So the answer is still no.' He walked across the room to stand by the window, his back to her. 'Then this time I demand to know the reason why you won't marry me. That much you owe me.' His voice was hard, his tone implacable.

Sophie lay quite still, her head turned away from him, hesitating. Could she tell him? Did she have the courage?

'Well?' he demanded. 'I'll wait here all night if need be. The door is locked and I have the key.'

At that her head rose sharply.

'There's no need to threaten me,' she snapped angrily. 'Threats won't make me tell you just as blackmail won't persuade me to marry you. When I do things they're done of my own free will, not because I'm being bullied.'

'Bravo!' He smiled at her with that special light in

his eyes and she felt her resolution waver. 'So, tell me.'

Draping a sheet round herself, Sophie got up. Max uttered an impatient exclamation and walked past her, coming back a moment later with a second robe. She belted the dark blue towelling round her waist, the faint scent of him rising pleasurably to her nostrils. Standing before him she raised her eyes to his face.

'My mother died shortly after my birth,' she began tonelessly. 'I don't know who my father was and I'm probably illegitimate. I was adopted as a baby and my name is that of the couple who adopted me.'

She was surprised to see anger in his eyes.

'Are you telling me this is why you've put us both through the unhappiness of the past weeks?' he demanded angrily. 'Did you imagine I'd turn away from you because you're adopted? It's you I want to marry, not your ancestors. And this does happen to be the twentieth century—in case it's slipped your mind. We're no longer in the Dark Ages!'

'There's more,' she said woodenly. 'I can't have children.'

'Max couldn't hide his reaction. She saw the shock in his eyes. He reeled with it. And then he turned away. She watched him swallow and saw his jaw clench.

The silence seemed endless, and she turned to stare blindly out at the beauty of the starlit night.

'Have you been to doctors, had the usual tests?' he demanded harshly.

She wished he would stop asking questions. She was finding it hard to keep cool, to answer him with any composure. Too much had happened too quickly and she felt giddy and weak.

'It's not that I'm physically incapable of having . . . children.' She blushed faintly. 'There's a disease in my family that makes it impossible.'

'What disease?'

'Please, Max, I don't want to go on with this,' she begged him.

'I don't care a damn what you want. I intend to hear it all.'

'Can't you just accept what I've told you?' she pleaded.

'No, I can't. This is not some interesting debate. It's about us—you and me.' He paused, his face grim. 'What disease?' he repeated.

'It's not fatal,' she prevaricated.

'And you have it?'

'No.'

'For God's sake, Sophie, what is this? You can't have children and then it turns out you can; there's a disease that might stop you, but you don't have it. Are you trying to drive me mad?' He breathed deeply. 'Just start again and explain it properly.

'Please, Max, can't we leave it at that?' she appealed to him, her voice faltering.

'No.' He brought his fist crashing down on the table in front of him and she jumped with shock. She had never seen him violent. 'Will you stop dithering and tell me—now! And I warn you, I'm fast losing control.'

She rammed her hands into the pockets of the robe, her neck muscles rigid with tension, her face drained of colour.

'It seems my father had an illness which can be inherited,' she said painfully. 'If I had children I could pass it on to them.'

'What illness?' he demanded again, and she could

see his store of patience was rapidly coming to an end.

'I don't know,' she confessed miserably.

'You don't know?' he echoed. 'For God's sake, Sophie, make some sense! How could you find out about this mysterious illness when you don't know who your father was, not even his name?'

She took a deep breath and tried to steady her voice.

'When my parents told me I'd been adopted, I went back to the convent to see if I could trace my ... natural family. The nuns were very kind and told me what they knew. It seems my mother arrived at the convent already in labour. There wasn't time to get her to a hospital, and I was born within hours.' She clenched her hands, her nails digging into her palms. 'By the time the doctor arrived it was too late to save her. Before she ... died,' Sophie went on in a whisper, 'she told them she wanted me to be called Sophie and I had to be told I couldn't have children. The nun asked her why, and she explained about my father's illness.'

'Without naming it?'

She nodded.

'It seems an odd thing for a dying woman to say,' he said slowly. 'Could the nun have been mistaken?'

'She seemed quite certain,' Sophie said dully.

He swung round to face her.

'If I told you all this doesn't matter, would you believe me?'

'It would make no difference what I believe. I don't intend to marry ... ever.'

He began to roam round the room, and her eyes followed him wistfully. She had managed to tell him, and now he knew it all. Watching him stride about, she realised this was finally the end. They would not meet again. In the morning she would go and he would be relieved.

Pain twisted inside her. Had she nursed a forlorn hope that he would brush it aside, tell her he loved her and they would be married in spite of her revelations? Wishful thinking, she thought miserably, just more day-dreaming. It was better this way, she told herself bleakly. A clean cut without regrets. Nothing left unsaid that might nurture hope when there was none.

Max's face was shuttered and told her nothing, no smile or spark of life in his eyes as he stopped pacing and looked across at her. It had been a blow to him, too. He didn't speak and for that she was grateful. She wished he would go before she broke down completely and begged him to . . .

Abruptly he turned away. At the door he stopped for a moment as though to say something. Then he changed his mind. With a brief nod he opened the door and closed it quietly behind him.

CHAPTER NINE

SOPHIE sat huddled over the fire, the dog at her feet. The clock struck, and she looked up to see it was almost exactly twenty-four hours since she had left Max's bedroom. And here she was, all thought of leaving the castle long gone.

It had been a bad night. She had not slept, dozing fitfully before dawn and waking with her decision made. She would make her apologies to her hostess and leave, explaining quite truthfully that she saw no point in staying. She had rung the airport to confirm her return reservation and then made her way downstairs to get help with her suitcase and find some breakfast.

On her way down she had been vaguely aware of a certain disarray. Cleaning materials littered the stairs apparently abandoned, and she could hear voices from somewhere raised in nervous argument. When she reached the hall the Rottweiler was whining. Uncertain what to do, Sophie sat down next to the dog, touching him softly and murmuring to him in German. He responded to her fingers and lay down at her feet, his head between his paws. Absently she noticed that the fireplace had not been cleared of yesterday's ashes.

Suddenly Frau Glaser appeared along the corridor. '*Ach, mein Gott,*' she said when she saw Sophie. 'I am so sorry. Your breakfast, it has not been brought up.' She'd been crying. Her eyes were red and she clutched a large handkerchief in one hand. 'We are all up and down,' she said, trying to make herself understood in English, forgetting that Sophie could speak German.

'Can I help?' Sophie asked. 'Is something wrong?'

Frau Glaser proceeded to wring her hands. 'It is the *Herrin*—the mistress!' she wailed loudly.

'Please, Frau Glaser,' Sophie said quietly, taking the older woman's hand, 'can we go and sit down—in the hall perhaps—and you tell me about it.'

'In the hall?' She looked shocked. 'Certainly not! I cannot sit in the hall. Twenty-four years I have been here and never I sit in the hall. It is not ...' She tailed off, her thoughts returning to whatever was troubling her.

'Something is wrong with the Frau Baron?' Sophie insisted gently.

Frau Glaser nodded, holding back her tears by pressing the handkerchief to her eyes.

'Please,' Sophie went on, taking her arm and leading her back to the hall. 'Let's sit down here, just for a moment.' Sitting primly on an upright chair, the other woman stared at nothing, almost unaware of Sophie's presence.

'It is always the same,' she said at last. 'She will not have the doctor.' Hopefully Sophie waited. 'It is the cough. It comes back in the night ... like last time. She has pain and fever, but she will not have the doctor. Before, the master was here and he brings the doctor. No nonsense. But he is away. Gone. And the Frau Baron says no doctor.' She was repeating herself, almost rambling, but Sophie waited, asking no questions. 'And Martha is stupid,' she went on, her voice suddenly angry. 'The Frau Baron says no, so it is no. I may not phone the doctor.'

'Are you saying Frau von Hartog is sick and will not have the doctor called?' Sophie asked quietly.

Frau Glaser turned wet eyes to look at her. 'Yes,

yes, that is what I try to tell you. And we cannot find the Herr Baron. He has gone, Franz says. But where? The office do not know. And this morning he was not here, so he must have gone in the night.'

'Who is Franz?' Sophie asked gently.

'Franz?' Frau Glaser looked astonished. 'He is the secretary to the Herr Baron, of course. And he does only what he is ordered. He is just a boy,' she added dismissively.

'I think I'll just go upstairs for a moment,' Sophie said and got up.

'Oh, no.' The older woman reached out a hand to stop her. 'Martha, she will not let you see her. She is mad, that one. Jealous, possessive of her mistress.'

'We'll see,' Sophie said, and headed for the lift.

Upstairs, Martha was surprised to see her. She came out into the corridor closing the door behind her and glared at Sophie.

'The Frau Baron is ill. She cannot see you,' she said brusquely.

'I'm sorry to hear that, Martha. You must have had a disturbed night,' Sophie added diplomaticaly.

'I have no sleep, and that doesn't matter.'

'I wonder if I could see her just for a moment? I am a nurse,' Sophie added for good measure. It wasn't true, but she had undergone some nursing training and had considerable experience of illness. Martha looked as though she would explode with anger, but Sophie didn't change her tone or the mild expression of her face. 'I understand the Herr Baron is away and cannot be reached. I know you wouldn't like anything to happen to your mistress because the doctor wasn't called.'

Sophie watched her words sink in.

'My mistress has no wish for the doctor, so I do not permit him to come,' stated Martha firmly.

'Why doesn't she want him?'

'Because he will take her to the hospital—to die.'

'But why should she die, Martha? Is she very ill?'

Suddenly Martha had no answer. Her face went red with embarrassment.

'If it is only something small—a cold perhaps,' Sophie hazarded, 'maybe we can help her—between the two of us.'

'You will not call the doctor?' asked Martha anxiously.

'That I can't promise,' Sophie said gently. 'But whatever I do, I'm sure we can decide together.'

There was a heavy silence. Then Martha turned and opened the door. The room was suffocatingly hot. The curtains were drawn, the air stale and oppressive. As her eyes adjusted to the dark, Sophie could make out two huge tapestry screens set at right angles round an enormous bed. Walking forward cautiously, she could see the tiny figure almost buried beneath blankets and velvet coverings.

Then she heard the cough—and froze. Deep and agonising—she recognised it instantly. Turning to Martha, she spoke quietly.

'Please open the curtains.' She saw the other woman tense. 'If you value your mistress's life you'll do as I say—at once,' she said coldly.

As if hypnotised by Sophie's voice, Martha moved to the windows. As the light fell into the room the patient moved.

'No, Martha, turn out the light,' she demanded querulously.

'Now turn off all the heating,' Sophie commanded.

'No.' Martha spoke firmly. 'I will not,' she added.

'Very well.' Sophie faced her. 'If you don't do everything I say and at once, I'll send for Frau Glaser and have you removed from this room. This is serious and we have to act at once. I will also be calling the doctor.'

Martha's face set mutinously, ready to refuse. Sophie didn't speak. She waited. There wasn't time for argument. Looking up into Sophie's face, Martha made her decision. Without a word she turned and headed for the gas fire.

'Right,' said Sophie, 'now please help me.'

And they went to work. Twenty minutes later, the old lady was propped high with cushions, her bedlinen changed, the room aired and a fire lit in the hearth giving a pleasant warmth and a comfortable glow. She had managed to drink a little of the barley water Sophie had poured for her and the heavy bedcoverings had been replaced by light blankets and two weightless duvets. She still looked drawn and in considerable pain, but the grey look was fading, and for the moment she had stopped coughing.

On the telephone the doctor listened carefully and agreed her diagnosis might be correct.

'I will be with you in fifteen minutes, Fräulein Carter.'

Sophie had guessed correctly. It was pneumonia. The doctor gave her some medication and was adamant it had to be hospital. Meeting the desperate, pleading eyes of the patient, Sophie took her courage in both hands and argued. Was it possible to treat her at home, with careful nursing? He gestured for them to leave the sick-room.

'You don't understand, Fräulein Carter,' he explained when they were alone leaving the patient with a chastened Martha. 'I fear complications.'

Sophie bit her lip. 'I understand, Herr Doctor, and it is not my place to argue with you, but I had rather see a sick woman battle to get better than have her in hospital convinced she's going to die and making no effort to fight the infection.'

'That is what the Herr Baron said last time.'

'Last time?' Sophie was shocked. 'She's had pneumonia before?'

'No. It was bronchitis—two years ago. She was eighty-two. He insisted also she remain here. She had the best of care and survived. But this time I am not so sure.' He paused. 'The heart—there is a weakness there.'

'Can the decision wait till her grandson returns?' Sophie asked gravely.

'It is a risk.'

'Has the patient the right to decide?'

'My dear young lady, the patient cannot possibly judge the issue,' he said shortly.

Sophie was walking up and down, agitated and concerned. He was the expert. How could she oppose him? And in any case she had no right to decide anything. She wasn't even family. Seeing her indecision, he planted himself before her, his hands behind his back, his eyes looking up at her through steel-rimmed spectacles.

'You called me in,' he said, 'and I'm more than happy that you overrode this household to do so. I'm not sure who you are or what rights you have in this house.' He watched the colour rise to her face without changing expression. 'But you must appreciate that the decision has to be mine.' She nodded unhappily. 'We doctors do understand the psychology of our patients, you know. And I know full well how important it is in a case like this. So I will ask you one question, and when you've answered that I'll make the decision. Is that agreed?'

'Yes.'

'If I give you one nurse—and that's all I've been able to find so far—can you trust yourself to share the work when she will have to go off duty?

Sophie didn't hesitate. 'I will take full responsibility for my part.'

He nodded. 'Good. You've answered as I hoped you would.' Sophie smiled briefly, her eyes anxiously fixed on his face. 'For the moment, then, I'll allow her to stay.'

She breathed an audible sigh of relief.

'As it happens we're lucky. Sister Maria is highly qualified and very experienced. I would trust her as I would any of my young doctors at the hospital.'

Tremulously Sophie smiled, close to tears as he turned and picked up his bag. 'I'll check with my patient and then, Fräulein Carter, you are on your own.' At the door he stopped. 'By the way, please give instructions that the Herr Baron is to be found as quickly as possible.'

'It is being done,' Sophie said quietly.

The clock struck again and Sophie roused herself. It was time to relieve Sister Maria.

Sister Maria. With such a name they'd all expected a saintly nun with a smiling face and an angelic temperament. But her arrival had dashed such hopes. She was enormous, her uniform rustling with every breath she took, and she treated them all as raw recruits in a platoon where she was the drill sergeant. Within an hour of her arrival, the whole household was in fear and trembling. She took one look at Martha and barked orders that had that good lady rushing round to do her bidding. And she had stamina. In the hours that followed, Sophie's admiration rose by leaps and bounds as she watched her take over the sick-room and ensure that the patient had all the care a hospital could provide. At the end of twelve hours Sophie relaxed, knowing someone able was in charge and that she herself had only to follow instructions.

By the time Sister Maria went off duty for the first time in the early hours, they were on Christian name terms, a quick understanding having grown between them in their concern for the indomitable old lady fighting for her life.

A quick wash and she was ready, on her way along the corridor to the sick-room.

'The temperature is up,' Maria whispered. 'She's very restless. If you like I will stay.'

Sophie shook her head. 'I'll call you if I need you,' she said softly. 'I've ordered your meal. It should be up in a few minutes.'

And so the night wore on. Sophie took her seat in the half dark, her eyes on the face in the huge bed, knowing the coming hours would be critical.

She wondered at her own concern for the old lady. She didn't usually become involved with strangers. But she was full of admiration for the fight she could see in Véronique von Hartog. The pain had eased with the medication, and the antibiotics were doing their work. But the cough, when it came, with its pain in the chest, racked the frail body and endangered the heart. Each time it started Sophie was on her feet, easing the patient's position, holding her and murmuring soothingly until the paroxysm was over. Once, after a particularly bad bout, she lay back exhausted as always, but her hand reached out and Sophie took it firmly in her own, holding it till she saw the eyes close.

The doctor came and went, and night and day merged into one without any meaning as Sophie's own strength began to dim. Maria could catnap, but Sophie found she couldn't sleep. Lying on the camp-bed in Madame's sitting-room, she found her thoughts were with Max. Where was he? Why could no one find him? She had met his secretary briefly when he had come upstairs that first day to reassure her everything was being done to contact the Herr Baron. But there was still no news of him.

The night in his bedroom she preferred not to think about, but her memories refused to be buried. And her feelings were wildly contradictory. One moment she hated him for what he had done, the way he had humiliated her sexually, but the next minute she remembered his passion and tenderness, his gentleness and the ardour of his lovemaking. In the end it always looked as hopeless as she knew it to be, and there was little point in thinking back over it, making herself miserable. All she longed for was to go home. If only he would come back, she could leave, her responsibility for his grandmother at an end.

It was the third evening that everything changed. The doctor arrived late and looked exhausted, his eyes red-rimmed with fatigue. He picked up the chart and his face broke into a faint smile.

'It looks as though she's turned the corner,' he said when they reached the corridor. 'The infection's on the wane.' Sophie stared at him in dazed relief. 'Now we have to monitor the heart. She will have to be kept very quiet. No upsets. And we must hope she will sleep. That's the best medicine of all.'

The rest of the night passed in a euphoric haze. Both girls were suddenly wide awake, and Maria refused to return to bed. Seeing to the routine with which they were familiar, they smiled broadly at each other, and Sophie felt her spirits lift. The old lady would survive. That was all that mattered.

As the sky brightened, Maria sent Sophie to sleep. Weakly she protested, but Maria told her she was no use as she was. She had to sleep. And she did. As soon as she lay down on the truckle bed she closed her eyes and slept.

Véronique von Hartog smiled weakly from the bed.

'That was lovely. I can't wait for the next chapter.'

Sophie closed the book. 'I haven't read Dickens since my schooldays, but *Nicholas Nickleby* was always one of my favourites.'

'You read beautifully.'

'I get plenty of practice,' Sophie admitted.

'You'll enjoy reading to your own children when the time comes,' the other woman said softly.

Abruptly Sophie got up. 'I'll leave you to rest.'

'You'll come back later and have tea with me?' the old lady asked affectionately.

'Of course.' Sophie glanced out of the window. 'I think I'll get some air.' She walked over to the bed. 'Is there anything I can get you before I go?'

'No, thank you, child. Maria will be in shortly, I expect, with her pills and bits of machinery.'

Sophie leaned down and kissed the old lady gently on the cheek. 'I'll see you later then.'

Downstairs, Boy rose from his favourite place by the fire to follow her outside. It was cold and windy. The air was damp and smelt of rain. Soon the snow would melt and the dazzling winter sunlight would be no more.

Shivering in her suede coat, she walked briskly, the dog trotting at her heels. He had attached himself to her during the past days and now bounded ahead into the woods as if glad to be away from the confines of the castle. He was missing his master, Sophie thought drily. And he wasn't the only one.

It was five days since Max's abrupt departure and still nothing had been heard of him. And time was passing slowly. Strangely the urge to leave had left

Sophie. She was living in limbo, drifting without thought for tomorrow. And there was a strange pleasure in each day, almost a sense of excitement. It had started two nights ago when again she couldn't sleep. A second nurse had arrived and her duties with the patient were less arduous, but restlessness in the early hours had finally driven her to get up.

Walking through the dimly lit corridors searching for the library to get a book, she had opened a door to find herself in the wrong room. Pressing the light switch, she had been dazzled by the blaze from three gilded chandeliers as the castle ballroom sprang to life.

It rose three storeys high from the shiny parquet floor, across the centre of the room two large fireplaces faced each other, surrounded by a mosaic of brilliant blue Delft tiles. At one end the minstrels' gallery ran the width of the room, and at the other three tiers of windows rose to the intricately carved wooden ceiling which looked down on the golden cherubs swinging from the chandeliers. It was stunning—a room of startling contrasts and fairytale glamour.

Among the portraits, Max looked almost casual. Where his ancestors were surrounded by dogs, children and horses against a background of the castle, its woods and gardens, Max stood alone on the canvas, his cool gaze challenging the painter. His face was grave and a good deal younger, the mature man with his powerful good looks not yet evident in the sensitive, boyish lines of the youthful face.

Afterwards Sophie had no idea how long she sat gazing at the portrait, but when she finally climbed up to her room she fell at once into a dreamless sleep. Waking late, she threw back the covers with a new eagerness. She would explore the castle, imprint on

her mind every room of Max's home, storing up
memories to take with her when she left.

And she was amazed at what she found. There was
beauty and palatial splendour, but the castle was also
very much a home. Max's private apartments she was
careful to exclude from her wanderings, but the rest
enchanted her. There was the picture gallery with its
outrageous ceiling made up of small ornate mirrors,
gold framed and heavily scrolled; and the elegant
sitting-room belonging by tradition to the mistress of
the castle, a place to dream, with its pale blue walls,
blue and gold furniture, velvet drapes and an
exquisite escritoire where letters would be written
and invitations accepted. But best of all she loved the
library. Oblong and narrow, it was small, with
scrolled mahogany bookcases rising past a gallery to a
wooden ceiling. And in the window embrasure she
found a knee-hole desk where she could sit and pore
over books, pictures, prints and drawings that told
the history of the castle.

Taking her enthusiasms back to Véronique, Sophie
found the old lady delighted to regale her with stories
of the castle and its owners. Born at the turn of the
century, she had lived through two world wars, and
Sophie was riveted by the tales she told. It was the
second day that she talked for the first time directly
about her grandson.

'Very unpopular, our Max,' she said softly.

'That's difficult to believe,' said Sophie unthinkingly, and then blushed as Véronique looked at her
with an affectionate smile.

'You're biased, child,' she said softly. 'You're in
love with him.' Sophie didn't disclaim. 'Good,' she
added after a moment. 'I'm pleased you don't deny
it.' They were speaking in French to make communication less of an effort for the invalid, and Sophie was

quite content to listen, her only concern that she should not tire herself with too much talk.

'Unpopular?' she prompted.

'He's a loner, you see, and they don't like it here—in the club to which we all belong.'

'Club?'

'There aren't many aristocrats left in Europe, and those that remain stick together, especially those still in possession of their land. Mostly their estates are run by professional managers while the owners live the life of past centuries that can still be found in Vienna—balls, parties, the opera and all the rituals that belong to our class.' The old lady smiled sardonically. 'And Max does not join in. He doesn't even hunt, and that's a cardinal sin. Add to that that he's in his thirties and still a bachelor, and you have a man out of favour.'

She looked across at Sophie. 'He prefers his own company or that of a few close friends. That's why I'm so eager for him to marry. He needs a wife who'll be happy to adore him and run his home, bring up his children. A woman who wants to flaunt his wealth and spend most of her time in Vienna wouldn't suit him at all.' She stopped and looked at Sophie who was miles away in her thoughts.

Did Dorothea fit the picture Véronique had just painted? Did she regret marrying Klaus who did live in Vienna and presumably provided her with the life she lived now? But if he still loved Dorothea, as he appeared to do, why had he proposed marriage to another woman?

Véronique was lying back with her eyes closed, a curiously tender smile on her face.

'You're tired,' Sophie said. 'Time I went. It's enough for today.'

'No,' she said sharply, and opened her eyes wide. 'I

don't know what has gone wrong between you and Max, but this may be my last chance to tell you things you should know.'

'Please, *madame*, I . . .'

'If you won't call me *grand'mère*,' the soft voice interrupted, 'I wish you'd call me Véronique.' She smiled with sudden brilliance, reminding Sophie so vividly of Max that she felt her throat constrict with emotion.

'Max's father Johann was my oldest son,' she began, 'and at twenty-two he fell in love. She was young, the daughter of friends, and we were ecstatically happy. They had a wedding dreams are made of and came here to live. But it all turned into a hideous nightmare.' She sighed.

'Henriette was young and beautiful, but she was also vain and stupid, in love only with herself, interested only in her own body, how it was clothed and where it should be shown off.' She leaned back and looked at Sophie. 'It was hard watching my own son wretchedly unhappy. When Max's sister Eva was born, Henriette decided she would never go through another pregnancy. Since they were both strict Catholics it meant denying her husband his conjugal rights, and Johann couldn't cope with that. Another man would have turned away cynically and found his satisfaction elsewhere, but he was too young to believe she meant it. He courted her, spoiled her, spending lavishly and never leaving her side, neglecting his work. But nothing came of it, and the night Max was conceived I am convinced Johann inflicted violence on his wife. They never talked of it, but they never shared a bedroom again.

'When Max was born Henriette turned her back on him, handing him over to maids and nannies. And sadly his father also avoided him, because Max reminded him too much of the night when he had finally dashed his hopes of a normal marriage. When Max was two years old his father left home and we never saw him again. Shortly before Max's fourteenth birthday he died.'

She stopped and lay back.

'No more,' Sophie said firmly, and got up, leaving the old lady to rest. It was not until the next afternoon that the story continued. They had drunk their tea, and the room was silent except for the hiss of logs in the grate and the ticking of the grandfather clock.

'No questions, Sophie?' Véronique's voice came quietly.

'None. Today we'll just sit quietly and I'll read to you.'

'I need to tell you, child. Can you not understand that?'

'Not at the cost of your health,' Sophie said stubbornly.

'Time is so precious and I've so little left. If you understand about Max, it might help you make the right decision.'

Sophie didn't answer. The decision, right or wrong, had been made and was irreversible, she thought in sudden desolation.

'There's not much more,' the voice from the bed insisted. 'Please ... I need to unburden myself. You see, much of what happened to Max was my fault.'

'Your fault?' Sophie didn't believe her.

'I should have cared for him when his mother rejected him, but I didn't. I thought it wrong to interfere. My own mother-in-law had tried to run me when I first came here as a young bride, and I vowed I'd never try to rule my children.' Véronique paused. 'It was my husband—my wonderful Hugo—who took Max under his wing. Max was only a toddler when Hugo began to show him his inheritance, breeding into him his own love of the forests. Max is very like him,' she said softly, 'loving and gentle, but manly. Only Max has something Hugo never had. Max is ruthless. He wouldn't hesitate to sweep everything before him to get his own way.'

She sat up and Sophie plumped cushions and helped lift her to make her more comfortable.

'Did he ever tell you that he left home at sixteen to study abroad? It was entirely his decision, and he was away at university in Canada for four long years, studying the greatest forests in the world. And all that time we never saw him. Where other students returned home in the summers, he stayed labouring in the lumber camps, learning to speak English better than most Englishmen.' The old lady smiled to herself.

'He went away a rather lonely teenager. When he came back he was a man, virile and mature, his perception of people acute beyond his years. He was able to handle men who worked for him better than others twice his age.' She turned to Sophie and smiled. 'Hugo was astounded. Where was the sensitive boy we'd sent out into the world? We never saw him again, and somewhere in those years his ruthlessness was born. I didn't notice at first, but then one night it stared me in the face.'

She breathed in deeply.

'It was the evening of the spring ball. Each year we give a ball at the start of the Salzburg Easter Music Festival. And I was proud of my grandson, handsome and tall in evening dress. Seeing the many beauties on parade, I hoped he might choose one of them and settle down. Instead I learnt a lesson I have never forgotten.'

Sophie gazed at her, totally absorbed in what she

was being told, learning at last something about the man she loved.

'I watched in amazement as the women threw themselves at him, some brazen, others casting longing looks, hoping to be noticed. And each one he put in her place, politely, with charm and totally without compunction. I was horrified ... frightened. So young and yet so ruthless. And I agonised that night over what might become of him. Since that evening nothing has happened to reverse my opinion or allay my fears for him. Until now.'

'I know,' Sophie said quietly, 'only I'm not beautiful.'

'Oh, no, my dear,' Véronique said firmly. 'I was quite wrong about that. Your beauty is there, waiting, and once you're happy it will blossom and everyone will see it.'

Sophie blushed.

'What of his mother?' she asked. 'What happened to Henriette?'

There was such a long pause that Sophie wondered if Véronique had heard her.

'While Max was in Canada,' came the soft reply, 'Henriette left us to enter a convent. That was fifteen years ago. Since then she has refused all visitors, sent back our letters and never leaves the convent. As far as we know, she's still alive.'

CHAPTER TEN

IT was raining, and Sophie dashed up the driveway to the castle. Her walk had done her good, blowing away cobwebs that had been gathering over the last week. In the vestibule she took off her boots as Boy shook his wet body. Inside the hall the fire greeted them and the dog made a beeline for his favourite spot by the blaze.

She had been out longer than she intended, and it was time to change and join the invalid for tea. Striding along the corridor, she waited for the lift. It came to a stop, the doors opened and Max stepped out into the corridor.

For a moment Sophie stood speechless, gazing up at him, thinking she must be dreaming as she had done so often in the last few days. But then he moved and she stepped forward into his arms with a cry of gladness.

'You've come,' she whispered. 'You've come back!'

'Oh, my dear,' he breathed softly, holding her close.

'Have you seen her?' she asked, her voice muffled against his chest.

'Yes, I have.' He was stroking her hair, gentle fingers threading it back from her face, and she felt a rush of happiness at his nearness. 'She'll make it now.'

'I know,' Sophie managed brokenly before her control suddenly gave out and she burst into tears. Sobs shook her as she wept into his suit, her fingers hanging on to his lapels. 'I'm sorry,' she gulped, and

161

felt his arms tighten round her.

'It's all right now,' he whispered into her hair. 'I'm here.' A large white handkerchief appeared, and he tilted back her head to wipe her eyes and dab at the tears on her cheeks. 'There, that's better,' he said softly.

She gave him a shaky smile just as a movement behind her caught her attention, reminding her that they were standing in the middle of the corridor in full view of anyone coming by. She turned round and the smile died on her lips. Standing in the corridor was Dorothea von Hartog.

Sophie froze.

So that's why Max couldn't be found, was her first thought. He must have left the castle that night and gone straight to Dorothea ... immediately after she had told him all about herself. Sharply she pulled away from him and stared up into his face as bits of information long forgotten came back to mind.

Emil had been so sure of his mother's love for his uncle. Was Max a constant visitor in Dorothea's home? Was that how the little boy knew all about their relationship—because he saw it day by day? Perhaps the whole fabric of her own relationship with Max had been an elaborate charade to deceive Klaus von Hartog? Dear God, it was all possible. The sophistication of the von Hartog family was way beyond her, she realised with sudden bitterness.

Dragging her eyes from his face, Sophie brushed past him into the lift.

'Sophie—wait!'

She heard him call out as the doors closed and then she was alone, being swept up and away from him.

In her bathroom she washed her face and stared at her reflection in the glass. She looked ghastly. Her skin was grey with fatigue, her eyes ringed with black shadows, her hair a mess and her suit crumpled. Listlessly she walked into the bedroom and sank on to the bed, her mind vacant, her eyes staring blankly at nothing.

She barely heard the knocking on her door or Max's voice calling her name. And eventually there was silence. She turned to slide on to the bed, burying her face in her arms as misery engulfed her.

When she woke it was evening. The telephone by her bed was ringing, and momentarily she was confused to find herself fully dressed on top of the bed. Then she remembered and reached for the phone.

'Hello?' It was Dorothea. 'I have to speak with you,' she said urgently when Sophie didn't speak. 'Can you meet me downstairs in the hall ... right away? Max has gone up to change for dinner and we won't be disturbed.'

'No,' Sophie said, 'I don't think we have anything ...'

'Please,' Dorothea insisted, her voice strange—as though she was pleading.

'Very well,' said Sophie curtly.

Twenty minutes later, refreshed and changed, Sophie came downstairs. Dorothea was sitting on one of the sofas, a magazine in her hands.

'There you are,' she said impatiently.

As always she looked impeccable. Every curl in place, she was wearing a cashmere skirt and jacket, a cream silk blouse and glossy boots, her jewellery sparkling on her fingers and round her neck, and suddenly Sophie wished she hadn't agreed to this meeting.

'I want to talk to you. Please sit down.' Dorothea

tossed the magazine on to a table and Sophie felt a quick flicker of dislike.

'I don't believe we've anything to discuss,' she said coolly.

'Oh, yes, we do,' said Dorothea grimly, and Sophie sat down, not wishing the servants to hear them squabbling. 'If we're going to share the same man, we have something in common, wouldn't you say?'

Sophie said nothing, her eyes fixed on the other woman as she waited for what was coming.

'Max can be ruthless, as we all know,' Dorothea went on, 'but in some ways he's soft as butter, and I have this feeling he hasn't yet told you the truth about this marriage of yours.'

Sophie tensed, her hands clenched in the pockets of her skirt.

'I'm getting a bit bored with the delay,' Dorothea continued, her eyes on the perfection of her nails. 'After all, we've known since Kitzbühl about the annulment.' She looked at Sophie's frozen face and stopped in surprise. 'You don't know what I'm talking about, do you?'

When Sophie didn't speak she sighed impatiently.

'So I was right. He hasn't told you. I'd better fill you in,' Dorothea said bluntly. 'Max has been hoping for an annulment of my marriage so that we can be married in church. But that has now been refused, so Max has ruled out our marriage. But in a way it suits me better. He's not really good husband material, but he'll make a dazzling lover, and they'll be green with envy in Vienna when they find out I've snaffled him.' She smiled to herself. 'Anyway, in Kitzbühl I had this brilliant idea. You were obviously dotty about him, so why shouldn't he marry you? It would make his grandmother happy, give him the children he has to have and provide him with the respectable front so dear to him. He can spend time here for all the duties and ceremonies he thinks important, but our home together will be in Vienna where I want to live.' She looked up. 'It's really a perfect solution. And you're the ideal woman for the job. Not only do you love him, but you'd put up with his grandmother, you adore children and you're obviously a born little organiser and quite happy to be the mistress of this awful place.' She looked round and shuddered. 'My life is in Vienna, not this provincial village with its outdated lifestyle.'

She shrugged. 'I had some trouble persuading Max, of course. He has these terrible hang-ups. There's Klaus whom he doesn't want to hurt; there are all those damn trees and there's his grandmother. But I persuaded him in the end,' she added with a curl of her lips. 'So all he had to do was persuade you into marriage.' She looked across at Sophie with some curiosity. 'And it seems he's having difficulty with that. Normally he has no trouble persuading women to do as he wants, but for once he seems to be a bit slow getting there, and I thought a little chat between the two of us could hurry it along.'

Sophie hadn't moved; her eyes were riveted to the other woman's face watching every word emerging from that round pink mouth. When the spate finally dried up, she felt bludgeoned, battered by words that glanced past her guard, digging deep into the places where they could wound unbearably. Sitting quite still, she tried to ignore the pain, to figure out if it could be true.

It certainly explained Max's insistence on marriage, even his suggestion in Kitzbühl of a bogus marriage. And Dorothea was right. She herself was the ideal candidate for such a plan. Neither beautiful nor well born, she would be offered by such a marriage a life she could never have envisaged for herself. She would have a splendid home, money, a family and a handsome husband to stand at her side when needed. And to all that could be added the fact that she was no longer young, with dreams of romance addling her brain. Yes, it all fitted only too hideously.

But was it true? Was Max capable of such deceit? Could he betray the trust of his cousin Klaus, his grandmother? And was his love for Dorothea so strong that he was prepared to abandon his estates? His grandmother had told her how indifferent he had always been to other women. Could that be because of his secret love for his cousin's wife?

And it answered another question that Sophie had never openly admitted to herself.

Why me? she had asked herself countless times.

She had no beauty, no prestigious family background, none of the qualities to attract a man like Max von Hartog. So had he pretended to love her, convincing her of feelings that never existed? Had she been so gullible that she had never seen the reality, only what she hoped was true? The pieces of the puzzle suddenly fell into place, bringing the finished picture sharply into focus.

'Well?' Dorothea asked impatiently.

Sophie had nothing to say to this woman who had finally brought the last of her dreams crashing down around her. Without a word she got up and walked away.

Once more back in her bedroom, Sophie stripped off her clothes and stepped under the shower, scrubbing her body with vicious force as if to cleanse it. By the time she had rubbed herself dry, the pain was giving way to a slow, burning anger, so strong it was driving out the deep hurt.

Max had deceived her—lied to her. She said it out loud to her reflection in the mirror as she powdered and lotioned her body. He had traded on her feelings to get what he wanted—a marriage of convenience. Convenient for him! Had he been honest with her, telling her what he wanted, she would have felt some respect for him. But pretending to feelings that didn't exist in order to persuade her into marriage, she couldn't stomach. It made her feel ill, and her chest constricted with the familiar pain. But never again, she vowed. She had shed her last tears for Maximilian von Hartog. And she wished him joy of his Dorothea, who was brutally selfish, hard as steel, and would probably make him thoroughly miserable.

Sitting on a stool before the dressing table mirror, Sophie stared at her reflection. Nothing had changed. Beauty hadn't suddenly blossomed in her face. She had been gullible, she admitted to herself, stupid and naïve, all the things she prided herself she was not, falling into his arms at the first sign of male attention. But at least she'd been honest. She had loved and wanted him, and now she felt no shame, only anger. He was the loser in this little game he'd played with her, and this time she would leave him without regrets. And Lottie had been right after all. She was suddenly fiercely glad she had come. It was better to know the truth and learn to live with it.

Half an hour later she was ready, surprised at the image that smiled rather warily back at her. She had chosen the blue dress she had worn on her first evening. Her hair she'd left loose, brushing it into a thick mane of soft curls that just touched her shoulders. Her eyes she'd glossed with blue shadow that faded to her brows into glittering silver, and her lips were a brilliant red. She looked good, she decided firmly, and tightened the sash of her dress to emphasise the curve of her waist. She was ready to go down and face them both—for the last time.

'Here she is!' said Dorothea rudely as Sophie appeared in the dining-room. She looked down at the glamorous figure, tonight in black, and met the blank stare of those cold blue eyes. There was triumph in Dorothea's face and her mouth was curved into an empty smile.

Dorothea lacked dignity, Sophie decided suddenly. However impeccable her background, she had no manners, and where Sophie came from that rated very low. You have to have manners, her parents had taught her. Without them we'd all be back in the jungle. She returned Dorothea's look without blinking, her own eyes brilliant with scorn.

Max came across the room, his eyes glittering as he looked down at her.

'My dear,' he said softly, and lifted her hand to his lips before he pulled out a chair and she sat down. She tilted her head and gave him a wide smile. The colour rose darkly under his tan, and sudden triumph swept over her. Not entirely indifferent to her was the Herr Baron. Across the table Dorothea glowered, and Sophie felt an exhilaration that was highly pleasurable.

'Have you seen your grandmother?' she enquired of Max as she was served with soup.

'Yes. She missed you this afternoon.' He waited, but Sophie didn't respond; her face was bent to her plate. 'You couldn't make it, apparently,' he added.

Still she didn't comment. 'Did you find her better?' she asked.

'She's very weak,' said Dorothea shortly. 'I don't believe in all this kidding around. She's not going to get better.'

Sophie's spoon clattered into her plate and she turned shocked eyes on the other woman.

'No. Dorothea, that's not so,' Max said after a tense moment. 'She's weak, of course. Her system has to recover from the terrible strain of her illness, but most certainly she'll get better. She's strong and determined.'

Suddenly the other two at the table no longer interested Sophie. For a while she had forgotten about the old lady upstairs, and as the meal progressed, she took no further part in the conversation. When the dessert arrived she excused herself.

'I'd like to see Madame before she settles for the night,' she explained, and Max rose as she left the table. Tiptoeing into the sick-room, she saw Maria by the window, a shaded lamp on the table beside her, a newspaper open. Véronique was asleep, the pale face tranquil. Sophie hesitated. Should she wait? Maria got up and gestured for her to follow. Outside in the corridor they whispered.

'How is she?' Sophie asked anxiously.

'It's slow,' said Maria.

'But there is improvement?' Maria nodded. 'What about the heart?'

'The doctor's optimistic.'

Sophie sighed. 'And how are you, Maria? Would you like me to take over for a while? Have you eaten?'

Maria smiled. 'Yes, I've eaten, and no, I wouldn't like you to take over. I think you should leave it for tonight.'

'She was expecting me earlier and I didn't come.'

'I know. She was disappointed, but we didn't wait with tea.' Maria pulled Sophie's sleeve and led her to the sitting-room. 'I hear you're leaving tomorrow,' she said.

Sophie nodded and watched Maria bite her lip.

'I'm sorry to hear that,' said the nurse. 'Have you got to go?'

'Yes.'

'But you'll see her before you leave?'

'Of course.'

They both stood irresolute, aware there were things to ask and answer, and Sophie felt a sudden longing to confide in the other woman, but of course that was not possible.

'She has you and Martha, after all,' she said uneasily.

'She's become very fond of you,' Maria pointed out. 'You know of course she hopes you'll marry her grandson?'

Sophie flushed. 'I think she wants her grandson to marry and it doesn't much matter whom he chooses.'

'You're wrong,' answered Maria quickly. 'It matters a great deal. She's not bothered about great-grandchildren. She knows she's too old to enjoy them for long, even if they arrive before she dies. But she is concerned about him. She adores him and wants him to be happy.'

'I know,' Sophie said miserably.

'Perhaps you could play it down, tell her you'll be coming back, that you'll keep in touch—write to her.'

'Would she like that?' Sophie asked doubtfully.

'She'd love it.'

'All right, Maria, I'll do that.'

Maria left her, and Sophie stood in the hall. Should

she return downstairs and go through the meaningless ritual of coffee and saying goodbye? She had no wish to see either of them again. Her earlier elation was rapidly disappearing, and in spite of everything she was unhappy to be leaving. The castle drew her, and so did the indomitable old lady.

There was one more thing she wanted to do.

The small stool still stood by the fireplace in the ballroom, and the dog lay beside it as though waiting for her. He raised his head briefly to give her an intent stare before he lowered it to lie between his paws, his eyes watching her. She would miss him, too.

The portrait looked exactly the same, but it didn't draw her as it had done on other evenings. She got up and moved to the windows, her high heels clicking on the wooden floor. Outside it was dark, and her eyes blurred with sudden tears as she looked at the snow melting on the lake, small clumps of white bobbing gently on the water. Another month and it would be gone, the lake fully revealed, the trees on its banks bursting into blossom.

Hurriedly she turned away.

In her room the curtains had not been drawn and she stayed in the dark, depression now weighing heavily on her spirits. She must pack, she thought wearily, but didn't move.

A tingling down her back suddenly alerted her. Swinging round, she saw a dark shape on the bed and lunged for the light as fear shivered down her spine.

Stretched out on the bed, elegantly casual and supremely comfortable, was the master of the house.

CHAPTER ELEVEN

SOPHIE's breath caught in her throat and she stared at Max in disbelief.

'You've been a long time,' he said mildly, and swung himself off the bed.

'What are you doing here?' she demanded.

'I've come to talk to you,' he replied calmly, turning on the overhead light. 'Our attempts at private conversation tend to be rather fraught, don't they?'

'I'm not interested in anything you have to say,' said Sophie coldly. 'Please go.'

'There are things I have to tell you and I'm not leaving till they're said.'

'You're very good at making threats in bedrooms, aren't you?' she demanded angrily.

'What a lovely thought,' he drawled suggestively, and watched lazily as the colour rose to her face. 'You did rather lay yourself open to that, didn't you?'

'I'm not in the mood for humour.'

'I can see that. What's the matter, Sophie?' he asked quietly. 'Something's upset you. You were brittle as glass at dinner.'

'I don't plan to talk—or listen—to you ever again.'

'What's that supposed to mean?' He advanced on her.

'And don't touch me!' she screamed at him in genuine fear.

'Stop it,' he commanded, and took hold of her arms. 'Simmer down!'

'Take your hands off me, damn you!' she cried and lifted her hand to strike him hard across the cheek.

'You're hysterical,' Max said calmly, and hit her back.

Raising one hand to her stinging cheek, her fury boiled over.

'How dare you hit me, you arrogant bully? So you're a brute as well as . . .' She tailed off at the sight of his face.

'As what?' he demanded with icy rage.

'A liar and a cheat!' she spat at him.

At that he let her go, almost pushing her away from him and she collapsed awkwardly into a chair behind her. Looking up, she recognised that she'd gone too far. His face was grim, anger blazing in his eyes.

'Well,' he demanded coldly, 'are you going to explain that accusation?'

She didn't answer, and he turned his back and walked over to the window.

'So I'm a liar and a cheat,' he said heavily, 'but I'm not to be told why.' His shoulders were hunched, his head lowered. 'Something has upset you badly,' he said unexpectedly. 'I've never seen you erupt into fury and hysteria. I wish I knew who or what did that to you.'

Almost, Sophie softened. The quiet tone, the note of concern and gentleness had her melting again.

'Whatever it is,' Max went on evenly, 'perhaps it will help if I give you my news. I've been looking forward to it all day.'

He turned back to her and she noticed the tiredness in his face. It was etched in deep lines below his eyes which were now oddly glazed with pain. He dropped into a chair, his body slumped in weariness.

'I've spent the last four days in England.'

'Your business affairs are nothing to do with me,' she said coldly.

'Will you listen to me, woman?' he growled at her. 'I went to the convent.'

'Convent?' she echoed.

'Yes, convent. Where you were born—remember?'

'Oh.' She nodded, wondering what this was all about.

He leaned back in the chair.

'I discovered that the nun who'd delivered you died two years ago, and the Mother Superior is not the one who was there when you were born.' He sighed. 'So I decided to find the doctor who'd attended your mother. He'd left the neighbourhood, but I managed to trace him. He remembered your mother, but couldn't tell me anything. She was dying by the time he saw her and there was little he could do.'

He raised a hand to his neck, rubbing the tired muscles.

'So I followed a hunch I'd had while you were telling me the story.' He leaned forward. 'If you think about it, most women in your mother's condition would have made for the nearest hospital. But she didn't. She chose a convent to give birth, and I decided only one person could tell me why.'

'Who?' Sophie asked eagerly, completely caught up in what he was telling her.

'Assuming she was a Catholic, who was the one person she would demand to see before she died?'

'A priest,' Sophie breathed.

'Precisely.' He smiled faintly. 'It took me two days to track him down, but he did remember her. He'd been a young man at the time and had tried hard to persuade her to put the father's name on the certificate. But she refused. It took some time to get him to tell me the rest, but in the end he agreed to answer some of my questions because they applied to facts she had told him before her final Confession.' He raised his eyes to her face. 'I'm sorry to have to tell you your father died before you were born,' he said quietly. 'But it seems your parents were probably married. Both families disapproved of the match and they eloped. How your father died the priest didn't know. What he did tell me was that your mother was very young—under eighteen, he judged.' He paused. 'But the most important thing of all was that your mother never mentioned your father's illness. Neither the doctor nor the priest knew anything about it, and both men were quite certain they would have remembered.' He looked searchingly across at her. 'I think the nun made it up.'

'But why?' Sophie whispered.

'Who knows?' He shrugged. 'She may have thought your mother was unmarried and wanted to frighten you, to stop you going the same way. We'll never know for sure. In any case, I'd like to start investigations.'

'Investigations?'

'There are agencies that will handle something like this with discretion, and I want to try and trace your father's family now that we know his name was the same as your mother's. All this is not important to me,' Max went on quietly. 'I'd like us to have children, of course. But what matters to me is you and I—our happiness together.'

'But the family—the estates?' Sophie stared wide-eyed.

'Emil can inherit ... or one of my sister's boys. There are plenty of heirs and time enough to think about that.' He paused. 'It was for you I went to

England,' he said simply. 'I think you may want children, so we have to make sure it's safe for us to have them.'

At his words tears started to her eyes. She was bewildered, confused. Why had he taken all that trouble to trace her family, to check her story? Was it because of the marriage he and Dorothea had planned? It certainly wouldn't take place if there could be no children, and that could explain his trip. But now he said he wasn't bothered if they had no children. None of it made sense, and she couldn't seem to put the pieces together. And her anger was melting away. Face to face with him, watching the unguarded eagerness in his eyes, it was difficult to believe what Dorothea had told her.

How could this understanding gentle man be capable of such tortured planning, such deliberate deception? Unhappily she turned her head away. She didn't know what to think.

'I see we're back with my being a cheat and a liar,' Max said softly. 'Can you tell me about that now?'

Sophie hesitated. 'Thank you for going to England for me,' she said finally. 'I'm truly grateful for all the trouble you took. But it doesn't change anything. I still go tomorrow.'

'So you fling accusations at me and I'm not to be told what it's all about?' He turned his back to her. 'Very well, I'll have to find out in my own way. I'll start with my grandmother and work my way round the household till I find out who's upset you.'

'No, Max!' She was horrified. 'You know your grandmother mustn't be upset.'

'So you do care about someone.' He rounded on her. 'It just happens it's not me.

'I . . . I hate scenes, especially pointless ones. When

I've gone, of course you must do as you think best.'

'Bargaining, are we?' he drawled.

'Certainly not. This isn't a game.'

'I'm glad you realise it,' he said angrily. 'It happens to be my future you're playing with so lightly.'

Suddenly he sighed. 'I'm very tired, Sophie. I've had a hellish four days and I'm not in the mood for guessing games. Either you tell me what it's all about or I'll throttle it out of you.'

He was standing over her and she should have been frightened, but his words were so childish and he looked so cross and weary, she wanted to reach up and caress his face. Hurriedly she looked away. Why did he still have this power to rouse her to tenderness? And what had happened to her anger? Suddenly she didn't know whether to laugh or to cry.

'Come on, cry,' he said, as usual acutely perceptive of her mood. 'Your tears I can handle. God knows I'm getting enough practice. I've never met such a girl for weeping!'

'I never cry,' she said crossly. 'Normally,' she added irritably.

His lips twitched. 'I'm glad you told me. I might never have known.'

'Stop it, Max. Teasing me won't change anything.'

'Nothing will be changed by whatever's bugging you. I love you and we're going to be married.'

'No,' she said, her voice low and vehement. 'I'm not marrying you. I don't love you,' she lied firmly.

'What?' In one stride he was at her side, his hands gripping her arms. 'We'll see about that!'

Sophie guessed what was coming and twisted in his hold to free herself. If he kissed her she would be lost to all sense and reason. He bent his head, and as his mouth touched her lips she bit him hard. He cursed loudly and let her go. She stumbled away from him and headed for the door.

'You vixen!' he muttered, and came after her. Taking her in his arms, he held her hard against him. 'That's enough,' he commanded. 'Quieten down and I'll let you go.'

She drew back sharply as she felt his breath on her hair and the warmth of his body against hers.

'I'm spattering your hair with blood,' he said suddenly, and she smiled weakly. 'That would be a good memento, wouldn't it?' For a second his arms tightened and then he released her. Keeping one arm round her shoulders, he walked her over to the bed and sat her down. Taking a chair opposite, he pulled out a handkerchief and dabbed at his mouth. 'I may never be the same again,' he said, and smiled at her. She dropped her eyes.

'I think I've mentioned that I've known quite a few women,' he mused.

'Several times,' she commented acidly.

'Wait for it,' Max stopped her. 'You might even say I don't go round emotionally blinkered, blind to what women feel and think.'

'So?' she enquired coldly.

'At the risk of sounding enormously conceited, I have to tell you that you do love me—very much indeed. Only a woman deeply in love would refuse to marry me because she thought she couldn't give me children.'

Sophie blushed. 'People change,' she said woodenly.

'Indeed they do,' he replied promptly. 'That's why I have to keep you close to me and make sure you continue to love me. I have all sorts of plans for that,' he added with a hideous leer.

'I'm sorry, I can't appreciate the joke just now——'

'My dear, if I didn't joke, I'd be striding about foaming at the mouth and likely to do you an injury. It's a defence, and it's getting more fragile by the minute.'

He meant it. He was on the edge of violence: she could feel it in the tension of his body. She wasn't sure if she could cope with any more emotion, but she sensed he wouldn't let her go till she'd told him. She gripped her hands tightly together.

'Dorothea told me why you want to marry me,' she said tensely.

When he didn't comment she looked up at him. His face was clear of guile. He looked merely surprised.

'And why was that?' he asked softly.

Sophie shook her head and looked down at her hands.

'Tell me,' he said tautly. 'Now.'

And she told him. Everything. When she'd finished, he was curiously silent, his eyes fixed on some point above her head.

'Of course,' he said at last, 'it all fits, doesn't it? I refused to have an affair with you; I pressurised you almost from the moment we met, and only marriage or the pretence of marriage would do—and I came to London after you. Very clever. I under-rated her.' He looked down into Sophie's face. 'There's only one thing that puzzles me. Why did you believe her?'

'All the reasons you've just given,' she said miserably.

'And your feelings, your understanding of me—what happened to that?'

She sat uncomfortably silent.

'You believed I could deceive my grandmother in

that shoddy way? That I'd just snap my fingers and abandon the work I love? And what for? A woman who wants to do the rounds of balls and theatres to impress her friends?'

'No,' Sophie said tonelessly, 'because you love her.'

'My darling girl!' he objected.

'She's exquisitely beautiful,' said Sophie abjectly. 'She's an aristocrat and she's Austrian. It doesn't take any imagination at all to see why you'd love her.'

'God damn you, woman, don't you know anything?' Max got up to stride about the room. 'She's cold and hard. She's ruthlessly selfish and grabs whatever she wants when the mood takes her. I don't know what she's like between the sheets, but I can imagine. And it puts the shivers up me. Her husband who adores her she's managed to reduce to a blabbering jelly, and as a mother she's a dead loss.'

He stopped marching about and looked down at her.

'And you thought I could love her? Follow in poor Klaus's footsteps? What sort of a man do you take me for?' He leaned down and gripped the arms of her chair. 'And that's another thing. Can you really believe I'd do something so hideous to hurt my cousin, a man I love and admire, who's been my friend since childhood?'

She didn't answer, nor did she look up at him.

'That's all very well,' she said, her voice low, 'but there was a time when you loved her.'

'So she took you back as far as that, did she? Yes, I had a crush on her in my teens. She was a girl with blue eyes and blonde pigtails. At that age that's all it takes, and I'm certainly not going to apologise for it. But it faded on the wind.' He straightened up. 'In Canada I met some real women and never gave her a thought. When I came back she was married to Klaus, and I never envied him. I could see her for what she was.'

For a moment Sophie sat uncomfortably silent.

'Whatever you say, I know I don't compare with her—in other things,' she whispered. 'I'm . . . I've no . . . real experience of . . . life.' She swallowed. 'There are things I haven't told you that . . .'

'Hush,' Max said softly, and put two fingers across her lips. 'Just stop right there.' He pulled her up into his arms and held her gently.

'You don't understand . . .'

'Oh, but I do. I understand perfectly.' He sighed lightly against her hair. 'Come, let's sit down.'

He pulled her down with him to sit on the edge of the bed. 'You thought I'd fallen in love with Nanny Carter, didn't you? The cool, composed, apparently mature woman.' He bent his head to search her face. 'But you see, I didn't. I fell in love with the girl underneath all that starch, a girl with fire and passions that frighten her because they might leap out of her control.'

'How did you know?' she whispered, her eyes huge and dark in her face.

'This,' he said, and took her lips in a swift hard kiss. 'It's all there,' he whispered throatily, 'and all mine—dammed up and waiting to pour out just for me.' He rubbed his thumb softly against her lower lip. 'That mouth gives you away.' He took both her hands in his and smiled into her eyes. 'And don't forget I've had you in my bed—alas very briefly, but long enough to know the wildness is there.' She blushed.

'Then you weren't disappointed?' she asked awkwardly, her voice low, her eyes lowered away from him.

'Dear God, Sophie, don't you know how I long for you? I've never wanted a woman so desperately before, and I can't handle it. I'm afraid of hurting you and yet I long for you.' He pulled her close and buried his face in her hair. 'I don't know how I've managed to wait so long,' he whispered.

'Then you do know I . . .'

'That I'm going to be the first?' He trailed his fingers gently through her hair. 'I was almost sure last week—in my room.'

'And you . . , don't mind . . .?'

'Ah, Sophie, don't you know it's every man's dream to be first with the woman he loves?'

Flushing deeply, she looked into his eyes, her own brilliant with happiness.

'You and I, Sophie, are going to be married. And soon,' Max said huskily. 'But tonight I want to show you just how beautiful you are. I'm going to make love to you—endlessly and slowly—as I've longed to do for numberless weeks. And tomorrow morning you will know how much I love you and you'll understand why you need never again fear any other woman.' He kissed her lips lightly. 'But first things first. I want all questions and misunderstandings cleared up. No more shadows and no more doubts.'

He lifted her hands to his mouth, kissing each one, his lips hot against her palms. 'Well?' he demanded softly.

'There is one more thing. Only it's silly really . . .'

'Come on, out with it.'

'Max, why did you want us to pretend to be married?' she asked softly.

'Ah, yes, the bogus marriage.' He smiled ruefully. 'I hoped, given a little time, I could turn it into a real one, of course. Even a child could have guessed that,' he teased her. Then his face lost its smile. 'Is that it then?' he asked. 'No more bogeys?'

She shook her head. 'No more.'

'All right,' he went on gravely, 'now it's my turn.' He lowered his head to regard her steadily. 'Look at me. Sophie,' he commanded gently. 'I have a question and the answer is very important.' His hold on her hands tightened, and she looked anxiously into his face, wondering what was coming. 'Have you any doubts about marrying me because of all this?' he gestured round the room. 'The life I lead?'

She looked puzzled.

'Life here is no picnic,' he explained. 'I have responsibilities to people who are totally dependent on me. Many of them have been here all their lives, some have worked for my father and grandfather before me, and I can never abandon them. They have nowhere else to go. Servants at mealtimes may sound grand to outsiders, but it has its disadvantages. Our privacy will always be limited, and pleasing ourselves may often have to be put at the bottom of the list.'

He smiled at her. 'I know from what has just happened here that you are the perfect mistress for this castle. No one I know could have coolly assumed responsibility for my grandmother as you did, overriding my household without a moment's hesitation. And from what Frau Glaser tells me, the staff here regard you already as their new mistress. So you see how selfish I feel in asking you to marry me? I'm taking—your warmth, your generosity of spirit and your courage. The selfishness is all on my side. That I will adore you and care for you seems a paltry return.' He bent down to kiss her hands. 'Do you still feel you can take me on?'

Sophie blinked away her tears and returned the

pressure of his hands. 'I love you, Max,' she said unsteadily. 'Whatever your life, I want to share it—all of it.' He lifted his head, and his eyes darkened with emotion. He said no more. There was no further need for words.

Carefully he released her and got up to close the curtains, turn out the light and put on the bedside lamp. Locking the door, he came back and kissed her softly on the mouth, his hands lightly on each side of her face. Then he lifted her on to the bed and, with infinite care, undressed her.

Sophie tensed, suddenly afraid. It was so like that other time. She was even wearing the same dress.

'No.' Max leaned forward and kissed her again. 'Nothing like the last time,' he whispered, and throwing off his own clothes, he slipped into bed beside her. His body was warm, and he held her against him, his lips on her jaw, at the corners of her mouth and trailing across her eyes.

His hands moved on her skin, his fingers conveying the pleasure he felt. One arm beneath her, he caressed the soft skin of her neck while his mouth travelled down her throat. She was tense, almost fearful of her own emotions, holding on tightly to her self-control.

Slowly his lips moved down to her breasts, his mouth open to take her nipples, and she gasped as pleasure coiled through her. His mouth trailed down across her taut stomach, and she expelled her breath in a long sigh, closing her eyes, conscious only of the tantalising touch of his lips against her skin.

When his mouth reached her thighs, her control faded. She arched her body towards him and reached her hands to his shoulders. Parting her legs, he bent to touch her in the most intimate kiss of all, and shock ripped through her as pain and pleasure exploded inside her.

Her whole being was concentrated on the devastation of his mouth on her skin, her body writhing and arching beneath his touch, her voice crying out for release.

At last he moved, his mouth taking hers with burning passion, and she clutched at him, feeling the hard desire of his body, her mouth responding wildly, her body lifting to his.

Slowly and with infinite care he moved inside her, and she cried out at the heavenly feel of it.

'Sophie!' he gasped, his breathing harsh, and she raised her body to his, dizzy with pleasure and out of control.

When it was over he stayed inside her, his face buried in her neck, his arms round her.

'Oh, Sophie,' he breathed, 'you're so beautiful. Made for me, created to fit only me.'

They slept, but twice more in the night he woke her, and each time they found new ways to touch each other, Max showed her how much he desired her and taught her how to pleasure him in turn. And the night seemed endless till they finally slept as the morning light crept through the curtains.

No one disturbed them, and it was almost noon when Sophie woke. One leg lay heavy across her, and his arm rested on her waist. She sank back, blissfully content, watching his face in sleep. Briefly she wondered if it would always be this good, and then she marvelled at how differently she felt.

It was true what he had said. She knew now that he loved her, felt it deep inside her and sensed she would not doubt him again.

Of Dorothea she thought suddenly with pity. How

unhappy she must be to fantasise about Max.

'And this is only the beginning,' a sleepy voice teased her. 'Go on, admit it. You were thinking of poor old, ugly Dorothea.'

'Max!' she protested laughingly.

He grinned and turned her chin to look into her eyes.

'Well, Madame wife, are you quite sure you don't love me?'

Sophie thought for a moment, a frown on her face.

'Mm ...' she teased. 'I think I'll have to spend more time with you before I can answer that.'

'You will, will you?' he demanded. 'I can see the sooner you're shackled the better.'

'Possibly,' she mocked him, smiling widely into his eyes. 'But I think I might prefer an affair. After all, marriage might not be as good as this.'

'It was good, was it?' he laughed. 'So are we to have no more nonsense about who else I might love?'

'Well—not today, anyway.'

'Come here,' he growled, and pulled her into his arms. 'I can see I've succeeded in what I set out to do.'

'And what was that?'

'Driving out your demons,' he said calmly. 'This morning you look like a woman who's been thoroughly loved,' he added huskily, and watched her blush. 'And now I'll have a battle on my hands with an impudent wife.'

'Or mistress?' she suggested.

He hauled her over to lie on top of him.

'Now try that again,' he threatened.

'Yes, Max. Certainly, Max. Whatever you say, Max,' she said meekly.

'You're learning.' He twisted her arms down her back and held her. 'Now, wench, will you marry me?'

I still haven't had a straight answer. And it's time to get up and have breakfast and deal with our responsibilities before we get back into bed.'

Sophie looked down at him with grave speculation.

'Well?' he demanded.

'Last time you offered me your money to spend,' she pointed out. 'What's on offer this time?'

'My body?' he suggested hopefully.

'Done,' she said promptly, and bent to kiss him.

Six exciting series for you every month... from Harlequin

Harlequin Romance·
The series that started it all

Tender, captivating and heartwarming...
love stories that sweep you off to faraway places
and delight you with the magic of love.

◆

Harlequin Presents·
Powerful contemporary love stories...as individual as the women who read them

The No. 1 romance series...
exciting love stories for you, the woman of today...
a rare blend of passion and dramatic realism.

◆

Harlequin Superromance®
It's more than romance...
it's Harlequin Superromance

A sophisticated, contemporary romance-fiction
series, providing you with a longer,
more involving read...a richer mix of complex plots,
realism and adventure.